To Ash

DANCING WITH DANDELION

TARA GRACE ERICSON

*Every flower has
to grow through
dirt.*

Tara Grace Ericson

SILVER FOUNTAIN PRESS

Edited by: BH Writing Services
Cover by Cat's Pyjamas Design

Paperback ISBN-13: 978-1-949896-25-1
Ebook ISBN-13: 978-1-949896-24-4

To Beth,
For your sincere friendship and encouragement.
Grateful for you.

"The heart of man plans his way, but the Lord establishes his steps."

Proverbs 6:19

CONTENTS

Prologue   1
Chapter 1   7
Chapter 2   22
Chapter 3   34
Chapter 4   48
Chapter 5   60
Chapter 6   78
Chapter 7   97
Chapter 8   111
Chapter 9   119
Chapter 10   128
Chapter 11   142
Chapter 12   155
Chapter 13   173
Chapter 14   184
Chapter 15   199
Chapter 16   214
Chapter 17   220
Chapter 18   232
Chapter 19   239
Chapter 20   249
Chapter 21   255
Epilogue   260

Note to Readers   281
Acknowledgments   285
Black Tower Security   289
About the Author   293
Books by Tara Grace Ericson   295

*L*aura Bloom looked into the deep green eyes of her daughter, Dandelion. Or Andi, as she insisted everyone call her. Whatever she wanted to talk about, it was something Andi considered very serious. At barely eighteen, Andi was strong and confident. Sometimes stoic and always steady. She was a sharp contrast to the care-free creative of her twin sister, Daisy.

"Just help me get these lasagnas in the oven and then I'll have a minute."

Her daughter wanted to talk, which wasn't unusual. It was simply difficult to find the time. Between sports, dance classes, drama productions, and church activities—this was a busy season for the Bloom Family. The farm was growing nearly too quickly for Keith to manage. Hawthorne was off at college, and Daisy and Dandelion would graduate in a few short months.

She handed Dandelion the shredded cheese so she could cover the top, then pulled the aluminum foil from the drawer. They worked in silence for a moment. Laura took the chance to pray for the conversation ahead. With six daughters, she was still learning how to navigate the emotions that so easily overwhelmed them. Just last week, Poppy had cried, wondering why her crush only saw her as a friend.

But Andi wasn't the type to get hung up on something like that.

They put the three lasagnas in the oven—two for dinner tonight and one to freeze for the next time someone from church was in need of a homemade meal. Then Laura sat at the kitchen table and turned expectantly toward her daughter.

"What's up, honey?"

"Well, I wanted to talk to you and Dad, but he's so busy all the time. I thought I could catch you and then maybe him another time."

This sounded serious. Laura schooled her features to hide her concern. "I'm sure that will be fine." The farm demanded long hours, and while

Keith was careful to sneak moments with all the children, it was hard to schedule.

Poppy stomped into the kitchen with Lavender on her heels. "Mo-om, Lavender stole my sweater again!"

"No, I didn't. This one is mine! Yours is the green one, remember?"

Laura held up a hand. "Girls! That's enough. It doesn't matter whose is whose, right? We would be happy to share, right, Poppy? And we will be sure to ask. Right, Lovey?"

"Yes, Mom," the girls chorused before scurrying back toward their bedroom.

Laura turned back to Dandelion. "Sorry, sweetie. Go ahead."

Andi fidgeted with her hands for a moment, then folded them and set them on the table. She took a deep breath, then said, "I've decided I want to go into the Army."

It took a moment for her to register what her daughter had just said. She blinked. "What about college?" They'd been on three college visits so far, and had another scheduled next month.

Dandelion held her gaze, her eyes full of determination. "I've really been thinking about what I want to do with my life. You know school isn't really my thing. I don't love it like Poppy does. I just want to go and do things, you know? I want to get out of Indiana and see the world. And I want to serve my country."

Hurt sliced through Laura's heart. "You don't want to stay here?"

Andi shook her head.

"What happened to Purdue?" Visions of her beautiful daughter on the battlefield flashed before her eyes. "Are you sure about this?"

But her daughter had made up her mind. Even Laura could see that.

"I really am, Mom. We took this test at school, and I've been talking to the recruiter. I'm excited about it. Do you think you could be happy for me too?"

Laura reached out and took her daughter's hand. "Oh, honey. If you are sure this is what you want... Have you prayed about it?" She'd been praying for Daisy and Dandelion's college decisions for months, but she'd never considered the possibility that they wouldn't go.

Andi nodded. "I've been praying constantly. And I keep coming back to this."

Laura felt a tug in her heart. Was her trust in

God really enough? What if something happened to Andi? She wasn't sure she could do this.

But looking at Andi's bright, confident face, Laura felt a peace settle in her heart. If God was calling Andi into the military, then God would take care of her until it was time to come back home.

1

*I*f there was anything more frustrating than being dismissed for being a woman, Dandelion Bloom wasn't sure what it could be. As she watched her friend Monique talk with the mechanic, Andi resisted the urge to roll her eyes at his condescending tone.

"Well, Ms. Pritchett, your brakes are shot. Kind of important, don't you think?"

Andi narrowed her eyes. Internally, she mimicked his tone. *Kind of obnoxious, don't you think?*

She tried to look like she wasn't listening, scrolling aimlessly on her phone. But Monique was flustered and Andi was debating whether she should step in.

"How much will new brakes cost?"

"Well, if it were only the pads, I'd say about $500. But you need rotors too. So we're looking at about two grand."

Andi nearly choked. The nerve on this guy was unbelievable. Brakes and rotors on Monique's little Honda should be no more than a thousand. And that was generous.

But the slimy mechanic didn't stop there.

"Unfortunately in the inspection, we also found the brake line is worn out. Which is another thousand. And your battery is low capacity, which is another couple hundred."

And he was a sleezy liar, which would be another thousand.

Monique turned to Andi with a concerned look on her face before turning back to the mechanic. "I-I don't have that kind of money."

"We take credit cards."

Of course they did.

Andi pasted a smile on her face. "Could you print out the quote for everything she needs so we can look at it all at once?"

When he handed her the estimated repairs, Andi skimmed the list. Everything he'd mentioned was on there, along with the inspection and oil change

Monique had actually brought her car in for. And then there it was—air filter replacement.

She pulled Monique aside. Her friend had a worried look on her face, and Andi rubbed her shoulder lightly. "It's going to be okay. This guy is totally taking advantage of you." Monique had just bought this car. The previous owner had a dog and since Monique was allergic, she'd had the car detailed. Andi had even changed the air filter.

Which is why seeing that particular charge on the estimate was a major red flag. As if the ridiculously high prices weren't enough, now Andi had evidence that they were trying to charge for unnecessary work.

"Are you sure, Andi? I don't want to drive around with bad brakes."

"I don't want you to drive around an unsafe car either. But I also don't want you to pay an arm and a leg to a guy trying to rip you off. See?" She showed Monique the air filter line. "I just changed your air filter."

Her friend's worried countenance changed to frustration. "I hate cars. Why did I move to the suburbs? At least in the city I could just take the Metro."

Andi laughed. "It's going to be okay, but you should find another mechanic."

Monique nodded. "Okay."

Andi wiggled her eyebrows. "Want to have a little fun with this guy?"

Monique laughed. "Be my guest."

Andi pulled out her most innocent voice. "Thanks so much for this. The only thing we saw that you didn't mention was the air filter. You really think her air filter needs changed?"

The man gave her a victorious smile.

Andi wanted to gag. He actually thought he had them hook, line and sinker.

"Sweetheart, we wouldn't lie to you. I'm not in the business of charging customers for services they don't need. Jordan pulled it out and said it was nearly completely clogged. We'll get it taken care of for you, though. Don't you worry."

Andi squeezed the leather braided key chain in her hand. "That won't be necessary."

"You really should change it, ma'am. You can trust us."

Andi didn't trust him as far as she could throw him. She dropped her clueless expression. "Oh? Then explain to me how your tech in there," she jabbed a thumb toward the garage, "is claiming the air filter is dirty when I changed it myself two weeks ago."

The shop manager looked toward the garage in a panic and shifted uncomfortably. Andi waited for an answer. Let him squirm. These weasels weren't going to rip off her friend.

"We...Uh...maybe Jordan gave me the wrong information."

"Oh, come on. Drop the act," she checked his nametag, "Paul. Here's the deal. You'll stop ripping off women who come to your shop, or I'll call in a favor from Wendy down at Channel 5. She'd love to run an exposé about how your little shop pads the numbers by charging for unnecessary work and not completing it."

Paul stammered and stuttered and eventually tried to stand behind everything he'd quoted.

Andi stepped back and let Monique take over. Her friend rolled her shoulders back. "I'll be taking my business elsewhere, thank you very much. I'll pay for my oil change, but not a penny more."

Begrudgingly, Paul handed over the keys.

Monique linked her arm in Andi's and they walked out the door. Andi felt a bit ridiculous, like the best friends in a romantic comedy, strolling down the street full of sass. But Monique's worried look had been replaced with laughter and a broad grin, so it was worth it.

When they got to her car, Monique turned to her. "Girl, what am I going to do without you?"

Andi waved her hand. "Oh, come on. You'll be just fine."

Monique wrapped her arms around Andi, and she tried not to stiffen. Hugs weren't her favorite thing, unless they were from her family. Was she supposed to pat her on the back? Or was that awkward?

"I'm going to miss you so much!"

She pulled back from the hug. "I'm going to miss you too! But I'll come visit. And you can come to the farm. You'd get a kick out of my sisters."

"I know. It just won't be the same as having you right here."

"Well, I'm not leaving for another month. So don't get all weepy just yet," she cajoled. After all the years with her sisters, Monique's emotional display only made her slightly uncomfortable.

Monique laughed. "Fine. Just beware, you'll get all the tears and hugs when you pack up."

"I'll start mentally preparing now," Andi said dryly. One of her favorite parts about having good friends was that they knew behind her relatively stoic exterior, she cared just as deeply as they did. It just wasn't her style to let it show.

It would be hard to leave her home here in Alexandria. She'd spent twenty years of moving from base to base, but the last six had been spent here, near DC. It wasn't that she didn't like it here. Despite how she'd wanted to get away from Bloom's Farm twenty years ago, there was something about being home that called to her now.

Her military career had been rewarding and fulfilling. God had kept her safe and helped her find herself as she served her country. But she had been clawing her way up the chain of command for years. Plus she was tired of dealing with the inevitable macho attitudes that were apparently issued along with the uniforms during boot camp.

She had no doubt it was time to do something else.

She waved goodbye to Monique and got into the car. If she went straight there, she could get in some time at the dojo before she needed to teach class.

Andi knew she wouldn't change anything about her military service. It had allowed her to see the world, being stationed in Korea, Germany, the Middle East, and all over the US over the years. She'd learned more than she ever imagined. But it was a lonely way to live. When you moved every three or four years, it was hard to make friends.

The guys she dated briefly from the Army never lasted long—and she'd decided long ago that dating someone in the service would be counterproductive to her own career advancement. She knew enough about the system to understand the added complexity of trying to navigate two career ladders simultaneously. Outside the military, anyone she met while living somewhere tended to balk at the idea of following her to her next duty station.

She was ready to be done.

If only she knew what to do next. With the expansion of the farm over the last ten years, she thought she would have a good job running security. Aside from a few high-profile events, it would mostly be managing the security systems and bouncing unruly wedding guests. Easy enough, right?

It was the easy option right now. There was a place for her there to leave her mark on the farm, just like each of her siblings had done. It just made sense for her to go home after twenty years away. She'd briefly considered the idea that this wasn't the plan, but the unknown was scary. There had been periods of uncertainty in the Army. What would she be doing? Where was her next duty station?

Someone else had always made those decisions. This one was all up to her—and she had to get it right.

Andi parallel parked down the street from Alexandria Martial Arts, the dojo where she'd been training since moving to Virginia. The Army provided limited training in hand-to-hand combat, but Andi found she enjoyed the training and control required. After the introduction from them, she began searching out other opportunities to learn from various teachers over the years.

She grabbed her gym bag from the back of the car and headed inside. After a quick stop in the locker room to change, Andi bowed and stepped onto the mat to stretch. There were few people in the dojo at this time of day since the evening classes for the children hadn't started yet.

She transitioned into a series of katas, allowing her mind to still. She focused entirely on the repetitive movements and maintaining her form. When her body was warm and her mind focused, Andi moved to the corner of the gym dedicated to a couple of martial arts bags.

She repeated the katas, this time putting power behind the punches and kicks as the bag returned upright repeatedly for another hit. During one short resting break, she found the eyes of Master Roberts watching her.

Andi folded her hands and bowed. "Sensei."

He bowed in return and greeted her as his student. "Kohai." Andi admired Master Roberts's innate calm and control. She'd rarely seen him angry, usually only when someone disregarded the rules of engagement for a sparring match.

He gestured at the bag. "Your form is good today. But you seem distracted."

Andi nodded. "A lot on my mind. Only one more month before I'm officially retired." Retired. Seemed a strange label for a woman who was barely forty.

"Ah, yes. Then you're moving, right? Where was it again? Missouri?"

"Indiana."

"What do you need, kohai?"

Unlike some of her previous teachers, Master Roberts never pushed his advanced students, letting them guide their practice and pace.

"I need to get out of my head. Katas aren't doing it for me. Any ideas?"

Master Roberts bowed. "I can arrange a randori, if you'd like."

Andi bowed in return. A sparring match

sounded perfect. But who would Master Roberts match her with on such short notice?

Ross McClain dropped his bag against the wall and said a prayer to refocus his mind. He'd been on the road for nearly a month this time and it hadn't ended well. The episode in Denver wouldn't make the national news, but he knew the breach in security would haunt him for a long time.

Today, he was just grateful to be home. And even better, he was back in his home gym. He knew he came more sporadically than most students, but thankfully, Master Roberts allowed him to continue his practice when he could.

The sensei walked over, and Ross bowed with respect. "Sensei."

"Good to see you. What do you have planned today?"

Ross shrugged. "I wasn't really sure. I visited a gym in Denver a few times, but it was a little too Fight Club for me. Any suggestions?"

"Do you remember Andi?"

Ross racked his brain trying to place the name.

He glanced around the gym, looking for a man that might trigger the memory. "No, can't say I do."

"You up for sparring? The two of you would be well-matched."

Oh yeah. Ross hadn't wanted to spar in Denver because the wannabe MMA cage fight crowd tended to spar hard all the time. He wasn't interested in leaving the gym with a bloody nose or a wrenched elbow.

That wouldn't be an issue here. At their dojo, nearly all the sparring was focused on technique and form. It was the benefit of working with a live opponent that made it valuable.

"Absolutely."

Ross watched his teacher cross the gym and talk to a severe-looking woman with short blonde hair, pulled into a low ponytail. He squirmed when they looked at him. The woman shook her head and appeared to be arguing with Master Roberts. She looked back toward him and he raised his hand in an awkward wave. She looked back at their teacher and the tiniest of smiles crossed her features before she nodded, and then the pair walked back toward him.

Master Roberts introduced them. "Ross, this is Andi. Andi, Ross."

He wasn't exactly excited about this pairing. But

it was bad form to question your teacher. It wasn't like he hadn't sparred with women before. Even if they hadn't looked quite so angry or intimidating as this one.

He flashed a small smile. "Hey."

She tipped her head up in response. Not exactly friendly, is she?

Master Roberts looked between the two of them, then laughed to himself. "Yes, the two of you will pair quite nicely. I look forward to seeing what you can teach each other."

He stepped away, leaving Ross to stare awkwardly at the beautiful woman in front of him. "I've seen you around a few times," he said lamely.

"I'd hope so. This has been my gym for almost five years."

Wow. She had been around that long? The way she said it—emphasis on the *my*—made him territorial. He knew he was a sporadic practitioner, but the roster of advanced students wasn't that long.

"It's my gym too. For just about as long."

She raised her eyebrow at him.

He resisted the urge to defend his status at the dojo further. It didn't appear it would do any good. Perhaps he was already getting the opportunity to practice his control.

"I've been focusing on control—choosing the correct move and executing it with precision, without emotion." He couldn't read the flicker in Andi's eyes, but perhaps that was for the best. "Do you have any goals for our match?" It was always important to make sure a sparring match helped both fighters in their training.

Andi shook her head. "Today? I just want to get into the zone."

Ross nodded. He understood that. "Okay." He knew he could help by keeping a consistent pace during the fight.

A few moments later, Ross stood opposite Andi in the center of the mat. Each was outfitted with sparring gloves and foot protectors. Master Roberts stood between them, off to the side. "Standard sparring rules apply. No elbows, no headshots. Be respectful."

Ross bowed to his sensei first, then to Andi as she mirrored the actions.

He chose his first attack calmly, a simple kick from his right side toward her waist. When she countered easily, he jabbed with his left fist. She dodged, then came back with an attack of her own.

He settled into a rhythm of strike, counter, counter, strike. Trying to help Andi get into the flow, he didn't alter the speed or pace of the movements. When one of Andi's kicks landed with unexpected power, Ross took a step back.

"Holding back on me, Andrea?"

Maybe he could get under her skin by calling her by her full name.

Apparently, it worked. Andi attacked with a series of punches and kicks that had him blocking furiously. When they reached another break point, she spoke through gulps of air. "It's Andi."

Noted.

"Okay, Andi. Are you in the zone yet? Because I'm ready to see what you've got."

2

*A*ndi clenched her fists inside her gloves. Ross was everything she hated about military guys. That short haircut and cocky smirk gave him away. She just hadn't figured out which branch it was yet.

He said he wanted to work on control though. And apparently, he had no problem with talking smack while they sparred. She was used to biting back the snarky comments that came so easily. This time, she decided not to hold back.

"It's a good thing this isn't a battle of wits, Ross. You'd be unarmed."

He laughed away the insult and a smile tugged at Andi's lips. She lunged, catching him off guard and forcing him to compromise his center of balance to avoid the attack. She took advantage of his out-of-position stance and stuck her leg out low. It would be bad form to sweep someone's legs out during a sparring match, though she was sorely tempted. Instead, she stopped when her leg met his.

His smile was gone, and she saw the frustration rise. Good. What would he do now?

They stepped back and he nodded. Then he came at her with a series of quick jabs and kicks. Andi struggled to block them and felt the blunt impact of his foot against her ribcage.

"Come on, Andrea. You can do better than that. Keep your knees loose."

She glared at his unwanted evaluation. "My name isn't Andrea," she growled through clenched teeth. As she attempted to regain the upper ground, Ross continued his verbal assault.

"I know I'm handsome, but don't get distracted." She blocked his fist with her forearm and jabbed with the other hand. He deflected it easily.

"Just because your mom tells you that you're handsome doesn't make it true." It was true, but Andi wasn't going to feed his ego. It seemed enlarged enough already.

"Ouch, Andrea. You're going to bring my mother into this?"

Andi rolled her eyes. If he called her Andrea one more time, he was going to end up on the ground. "My name," she lunged again, "is Andi."

He dodged her attack and Andi's body pulled forward when nothing stopped the punch. Swinging and missing was worse than being blocked. She was desperately out of position and wasn't surprised when she felt the impact of his hand coming down on her back.

They both stepped back, panting lightly. Andi blew the strands of hair out of her face that had escaped her ponytail.

"Oh, come on. Andi has to be short for something." He let his eyes trail down to her feet. "And you are short, after all."

Andi glared at him. "I don't need to be tall to beat you."

He raised an eyebrow. "You'd be harder to predict if you juked occasionally."

"Didn't ask you."

He held up his hands in surrender. "Fair enough. Let's make it interesting. First to ten points wins."

She nodded in agreement. It was standard competition rules.

"If I win, you have to tell me your name." Andi's eyes widened in surprise. She avoided telling people her full name at all costs. How confident was she that she could beat him?

As if he could sense her weakness, Ross chimed in again. "I can give you a two-point head start."

That did it. "I don't need a handout. I'll beat you fair and square. And when I do, you'll teach the Little Tigers class at six o'clock."

He narrowed his eyes. "Fine."

They each grabbed a drink and returned to the center of the mat.

They bowed and then began.

Ross must have been holding back on her, because this time he was faster, more balanced. Andi was on the defensive from the start. Frustration rose, as it was only a matter of time before Ross landed a hit and gained the points.

Sure enough, a spinning kick to her waist gave him a substantial lead. They stepped back to regroup. The next point went to Andi, when she caught him out of position and struck him in the ribs. Back and forth they went, until it was 9 to 7. Andi needed a big hit—either a spinning kick or a leg sweep. But first, she had to avoid getting hit by Ross. He could win with just one jab.

"If you keep your elbows in, you'll be quicker off the blocks."

Could this guy be any more obnoxious? "I don't need your help."

"No one will think less of you for losing to me, Andi."

She shook her head and scoffed in disgust. "You could break a leg jumping from your ego to your IQ. Let's go, Ross."

Apparently her insult had confused him, because she caught him off guard with the first attack. Andi saw a glimmer of hope, but he blocked the kick just in time and landed a fist to her exposed stomach.

That was the match.

Andi sat on the mat and caught her breath. Well, dang.

Ross couldn't think of the last time he'd sparred with someone as good as Andi. She was competitive, he'd give her that. She also didn't have an ounce of friendliness or humor within her petite, muscular frame.

He grabbed their water bottles and sat next to her on the mat. He extended her water. When she reached for it, he pulled it back slightly. "Ope. A deal is a deal. Your name?"

"Did you say ope?"

Ross shrugged. "It's a Midwest thing." He'd been out east for most of his career, but his Iowa roots sometimes snuck out. He shook the water. "Your name?"

"Keep the water." Andi stood up and strode off the mat. She grabbed a gym bag and shoved her gear inside.

Ross kept his eyes on her as she marched outside. She didn't even bow to Master Roberts before leaving—a breach of protocol the sensei could call her on if he decided to.

Instead, Master Roberts walked over to Ross and extended his hand. Ross rose to his feet with the assistance.

"She's... a tough one."

Master Roberts chuckled. "Yeah, Andi doesn't like to lose. It is good for her though. You did well, McClain. You have been working on the katas I showed you?"

"Yes, sensei." In fact, he'd used one of those exact

routines in the match with Andi. "They felt almost instinctual during the randori."

"Good. Keep practicing. Also, I hope you don't have plans tonight."

Ross frowned. "Why?"

"You seem to have chased away my teacher for the Tuesday night Little Tigers class." Master Roberts smirked when Ross groaned.

"Kids? Surely she'll come back."

"I don't believe I would take that bet." Master Roberts smiled. "I told you, Andi doesn't like to lose. Plus," the sensei's eyes twinkled mischievously, "I told her you would cover her class if she agreed to spar with you."

Ross's mouth fell open. "You had to bribe her to fight me?"

His teacher shrugged. "I don't believe Andi likes you very much." Master Roberts chuckled as he walked away.

"I guess not." What Ross couldn't figure out was why that bothered him. He'd never seen Andi making small talk at the gym, never really seen her smile. He didn't know anything about her, except that she was a heck of a fighter. She was pretty snarky too. He chuckled as he remembered a few of the insults she'd tossed back at him while sparring. Most students stayed silent in response to his ribbing. Some even asked him to stop. She was the first to respond in kind.

Ross removed the rest of his gear and checked the clock. He had time to go grab a snack before the class started. Teaching the beginner class was not something he enjoyed. His work travel had always been a convenient excuse not to commit, but the truth was that wrangling a bunch of six- and seven-year-olds was not his idea of a good time.

Logically, he knew he'd been that hyperactive child once upon a time, but now he was essentially an old man. He'd seen forty on his birthday cake more than a year ago. Briefly, he wondered how old Andi was, then dismissed the thought. It didn't matter. If the past was any indication, he might see her briefly at the dojo, but otherwise? He was busy with work. Soon enough, the presidential election cycle would really kick into gear, and despite the fiasco in Denver last month, Ross's boss had told him to expect to be assigned to one of the main candidates or their running mate. That would mean at least four months of being on the road wherever that candidate had their headquarters and anywhere they had large events planned. Probably Iowa, which meant he'd get to see his mom.

He grinned. At least *she* thought he was handsome.

Two DAYS LATER, Andi was debating the merits of various shades of gray in the paint aisle of the large home improvement store near her home. The townhouse was being listed soon, and she needed to paint the main living spaces something other than the awful muddy beige they'd been when she purchased it.

Gulf Wing Gray? Smokestack Gray? Pilgrim Haze? It occurred to her that someone out there had a job description that meant they had to name a thousand paint colors.

She turned the paint chips over in her hand and mumbled to herself, "I wonder what they get paid."

"Hmm?" She turned to see there was someone down the aisle, now looking at her. Then she realized the man wasn't exactly a stranger. Her own surprise was mirrored in Ross's expression.

She muttered to herself, "Oh, for crying out

loud." Wasn't it enough that he was at her dojo? Now he had to invade her neighborhood too.

"Well, if it isn't Miss Sore Loser."

She narrowed her eyes at him. "Well, if it isn't Mr. Know-it-all. What are you even doing here?"

He ignored her and turned to the paint counter with a paint chip in his hand. "Can I get two gallons of this in eggshell?"

"You really should use a satin finish on walls. It's easier to clean."

"Who is being the know-it-all now?"

She frowned. He had a point.

He turned and leaned back against the counter, crossing his arms as he waited. Kicking one ankle over the other, he nodded at her hands. "What are you painting?"

She held the gray paint chips under the light. "My condo. Living room and bedrooms. You?"

"Guest room. My sister is going to stay at my house for a few weeks. I got all the boxes I've been storing in there out, but now that I can see the walls, I realized how gross they were. I think the people who lived there before didn't believe in supervised crayon use."

Andi bit her cheek to keep from smiling. She

chose Pilgrim Haze, deciding it was arbitrary anyway. "Two gallons in satin, please."

"Eggshell is cheaper," Ross said.

"Some things are worth the extra price," she replied stubbornly.

"You don't like me." He stated it matter-of-factly, as though he was completely undisturbed by the observation.

Andi shrugged. "Don't take it personally. I don't like a lot of people."

"Fair enough. But you don't really know me."

Andi considered his words. Had she judged him too harshly? She looked up at him and her gaze paused at his crooked grin.

Nope.

That swagger just reinforced her previous opinion. He didn't take things seriously. For Andi, that just didn't sit well. It didn't help that it felt like her heart was squeezed tight in her chest. This was so awkward.

The moment dragged on and Andi prayed for something to break the tension between them. Ross looked like he was waiting for her to say something. The man in the blue vest lifted two gallons of paint onto the counter with a couple of paint stirring sticks.

Oh, thank the Lord. Andi took the sticks and tucked them into her back pocket. Then she grabbed a gallon of paint in each hand.

"See you later," she said as she scurried away as fast as she could. She was done talking to him. Hopefully forever.

Ross got under her skin. And she didn't like it.

3

*A*ndi waved her badge in front of the gate at Fort Belvoir. For the last six years, she had been stationed here as part of Logistic Readiness Center. They handled a huge array of equipment, operations, and security for units around the capital and abroad—especially in active combat zones, which had become her specialty during her multiple deployments in the Middle East.

Sometimes she felt more at home in the desert than she did in the green hills of Virginia mountains. Some of her best friends belonged to the local population there, or to the allied countries she'd worked with.

Some men in her unit had retired and gone to work in the private sector as contractors, immediately shipped back overseas but on a different payroll. Andi didn't feel like God was calling her to that though.

She parked and walked into her building. Today was her last day.

Her friend Sarah must have been waiting, because she immediately grabbed onto Andi's arm when she walked in the door.

"I can't believe you're leaving me!" Sarah had been in the Army for fifteen years, and they had crossed paths a couple of places before being stationed here at Fort Belvoir together for the last two years.

"Oh, you won't even notice I'm gone," Andi said.

"Um, false. This place won't be the same without you. I'm not sure the whole Army will be the same without you."

Andi smiled tightly. It wasn't that she didn't appreciate her friend's words, because she did. But if there is one thing she'd learned over her career, it was that nobody was irreplaceable from a work standpoint. It was a lesson you learned quickly in a war zone. When one team member was injured or killed, it wouldn't be long before a new one showed up to take their place. Harsh? Perhaps, but Andi was nothing if not realistic.

"Thanks, Sarah."

"Seriously. There's a whole generation of young female soldiers who've learned from you and looked up to you. And now you'll be gone."

Andi stopped walking and stepped to the side of the hallway with her friend. She met her eyes. "And now they'll look up to you. Don't underestimate yourself, Staff Sergeant."

Sarah's arms came around her and Andi gave her a squeeze. She knew she wasn't the warmest or most open woman in the world, but Andi loved her friends —and her sisters—deeply.

"Okay, okay. That's enough of that," she joked. Her lack of enthusiasm for hugs was no secret.

"Fine. But I get another one before you hit the road next weekend."

"Deal." Andi's apartment was almost fully packed, and she'd begin the long drive home in just over a week.

The day passed in a blur of well-wishes from coworkers, a small going away lunch with her commanding officer and the rest of the office.

She finished some last-minute training for the sergeant major who would fill her post. After years of positions in squad and platoon leadership, most of her current job was essentially project management

—she oversaw the operations of moving people and equipment around the country and maintaining security standards and records. She'd been responsible for similar things when she'd been deployed, with the added stressor of managing it in a combat zone for soldiers who were on the move.

Being back at Bloom's Farm was going to feel like a vacation. Maybe she would open a dojo or something. Terre Haute was big enough to support one. Either way, it was going to be an entirely different world than her career in the military.

At the end of the day, Andi packed up the last personal effects from her desk—a photo of her and her twin sister, Daisy, snapped at her wedding, plus a few books, awards, and knick-knacks, mostly gifts from coworkers.

With one last sigh, she turned her back on her office, flipped off the light, and shut the door. She turned in her badge at the guard shack and drove away. Twenty years was all wrapped up, ended with a few forms she'd filed months ago. Sergeant Major Dandelion Bloom was officially retired.

∽

Ross HATED BEING in the office. If you could call this open room with cubicles an office. On the road so often, he didn't even have one to call his own.

"McClain!" He heard the sharp bark of Agent Gallo's voice from across the bullpen—the ridiculous nickname for this wall-less room.

He stood up and looked toward the door. Gallo waved him over and disappeared into his office.

With a sigh, Ross followed the unspoken order. This had to be about Denver.

"I want to talk about Denver."

Wow, shocker.

"Look, we need to talk to Rogers about this at the same time. We were both there, but he saw the guy. His description is the best chance we have to find him."

"The FBI team on the ground is running down the leads on the perpetrator. My concern is what happened and how we stop it from happening again. You're my guy. Nobody else on the team can see the big picture quite like you do. Walk me through it and we'll find the gap."

Ross shook his head. That made sense in theory. Problem was, he'd done basically nothing but think through what had happened since he'd heard the gunshot.

"I've run through it a hundred times. We checked all the event staff, and we had agents at every entrance and eyes on the security feeds. Unless there was a leak on our team, I don't see how they got in."

Gallo was silent and raised his eyebrows.

Ross leaned back. "You think we have a leak?" Oh boy. That was bad. Very, very bad.

"I came to the same conclusion you did, McClain. Even if we missed something in a background check, there is no way that guy gets in unless one of the door agents drops the ball. Whether or not that was intentional is what we need to figure out."

"How?" Ross steepled his fingers under his chin while he thought. "Have the FBI found the shooter entering the building on video yet?"

Gallo shook his head. "Not yet. There were four thousand people at that church. It's going to take some time."

"Okay. Well, we can narrow down the agents in question once we see how they got in. Shouldn't be hard to dig once we know where to look."

"I agree. Just watch your back. You're headed to Florida next, with Rogers and Claussen again. I'm counting on you to let me know if you see anything suspicious, okay?"

Ross nodded. "You can count on me, sir."

He stood and shook Gallo's hand before heading back to the modern desk where his laptop was currently stationed. Ross opened his email and began scanning the daily report when he felt someone come up behind him. He turned and found Agent Rogers sipping a cup of coffee.

"Hey, man. Did you hear we're going to Florida?"

Ross nodded. "Sounds hot." He hated the requirement that Secret Service agents wear full suits while on detail. Sure, they had plain clothes agents too, hidden in the crowd, but somehow he always ended up being a suit. Especially in places like Texas and Florida, where he would soak through his undershirt before ten a.m.

"Nah, it'll be fine," Rogers said. "Think we can swing a trip to the beach?"

Ross rolled his eyes. "Check a map, Rogers. We're going to Gainesville."

Rogers shrugged. "Road trip?"

Ross laughed. "Not for me. Last time I rode with you guys, you played that death metal music the whole time."

"Aw, come on, McClain. You're no fun."

That wasn't fair. Ross was fun, wasn't he? Or at

least he used to be. Rogers and Claussen were at least ten years younger than him. "We'll see. Maybe if I can be the DJ."

Claussen's voice came across the partition. "Maybe a little Johnny Cash."

Ross raised his eyebrows. "You're a fan?"

"Gotta respect the Man in Black."

Another week, another destination. When his team didn't have a specific protective detail, they were on loan to just about any region that needed extra hands. Last week, Denver. This week? Florida. But before they left for the Sunshine State, Ross wanted to get the painting done.

That weekend, he reached down to grab the cans and zeroed in on the gray dab of paint left on the lid by the employee and one corner of his cheek lifted.

Ross looked at the paint chip sitting on top of the cans. Sea Breeze was a cheery pale blue color. Well, wasn't that a funny turn of events? He'd set the gallons of paint in the garage when he got home, his mind still on beautiful Andi with the stubborn streak.

Somehow, he had a feeling she wouldn't be quite so amused. He could go back to the home improvement store and buy new paint. No doubt that was what Andi had already done if she had discovered the mistake.

Instead, he pulled out his phone.

"Hey, Sensei. It's Ross.

"What's up, McClain? You coming in today?"

"I hope to later, but I wanted to get some work around the house done first. Actually, I was wondering if I could have Andi's number?"

Ross could almost hear the eyebrow raise through the connection. He felt the need to explain. "We ran into each other at the hardware store the other day and we ended up with each other's paint color. Just hoping to arrange a swap."

"Sure, sure. That seems reasonable." A hint of laughter colored Roberts's tone.

Ross loved to make people laugh, but he hated being laughed at. "Can you share it or not?"

He could hear the sensei's laughter. "I probably shouldn't, but I'm eager to see how this plays out."

Ross bit back a sarcastic comment and waited for the number. When he had it written down, he hung up the phone and stared at it. This was probably a terrible idea. Andi wouldn't like that he reached out.

He just needed his paint.

At least, that's what he would keep telling himself.

He saved her in his contacts as Andi and tapped out a message.

RM: This is Ross. We got our paint switched at the hardware store. Can we arrange a swap?

There. That seemed safe enough.

He busied himself taping the trim work in the guest room instead of staring at the phone waiting for a response. An hour later, the phone buzzed.

A: Of all the hardware stores in all the towns in all the world...

He smiled at the Casablanca reference.

A: Fine. I'll leave it at the dojo next time I'm there.

Ross frowned. It was a perfectly passable solution, but he didn't like it. He wanted to paint today, that was all.

RM: I'm trying to finish today. Can't I just meet you somewhere?

A: I'm busy.

He scoffed.

RM: Prove it.

Laughter exploded from his mouth before he could stop it when he saw the picture she sent. She'd taken a photo of herself. In the background, he could see empty flower pots, potting soil, and tons of vibrant flowers. It was Andi's scowl and sweaty, dirty face that got him though.

A: It'll be a while before I dig my way out of this.

RM: Shoot me your address and I'll swing by.

The message was typed and sent before Ross had a chance to think better of it.

She didn't respond immediately, and Ross began to regret the impulsive offer. She wouldn't want to give her address out to just anyone.

He began to type again. Maybe they could meet tonight instead. Then she responded.

He stared at the address for a moment. Just a few streets away. Somehow, he and Andi had existed in the same sphere for years and never met. Why was that?

RM: I'll be over in ten.

HAD she really just given her address to the egotistical guy from her dojo? Perhaps she'd been in the sun for too long.

When the car pulled up ten minutes later, Andi raised her eyebrow at the sensible sedan. That hadn't been what she expected. Ross grabbed two gallons of paint from the trunk and held them up.

"I come in peace."

Andi was wrist deep in a flower pot, pushing

around the dirt to make room for the fortune she'd just spent on plants her realtor insisted would help the curb appeal of her house. She knew they wouldn't last long. Her given name seemed almost fitting when it came to Dandelion's black thumb. The pesky yellow weeds were about the only thing that she could keep blooming during the summer.

"Give me a second and I'll go grab yours."

"No hurry."

She pulled the carton off one last petunia and squeezed it into the pot.

"Big project," Ross commented.

She brushed her hands off and pushed herself to her feet. Her knees ached from kneeling in front of the planter. "Worst part will be spreading the landscaping rock." She jerked a thumb to the pile of river rock in her driveway.

Ross winced. "Ooh, yeah. I hope you've got a wheelbarrow."

She nodded. "I'll be fine."

He looked back at the pile and then at her. "I could... If you wanted some help, I'm pretty cheap labor. Pizza usually does it."

She bit back a smile. "Thanks for the offer, but I got it. I'll just go grab your paint."

When she'd gotten the text message, she'd immediately run to check the color of the paint in her garage. Then she remembered the way she'd grabbed the paint from the counter and stalked off. How embarrassing.

He wasn't so bad. Maybe she was overreacting.

When she got back, Ross was surveying her landscaping project. "You know, if you bought perennials, you wouldn't have to replant these beds each year."

And there it was—the flash of irritation that inevitably came with someone telling her how to do something. "Obviously." She bit back the explanation of why she was choosing the cheap, colorful annuals. She didn't have to justify her decisions. If there was anything Andi knew how to do, it was to speak when needed and stay quiet otherwise. For some reason, Ross got under her skin and made it especially hard.

"Here's your paint." She offered the cans with what she was sure was an unfriendly expression. Andi didn't mean to, but unless she was purposely smiling, her default expression was one her friends described as resting brat face. She wasn't trying to be mean to Ross, but she also wasn't trying to be warm and fuzzy.

Apparently, he got the hint, because he dropped

the landscaping advice and grabbed the paint from her. He held it up awkwardly. "Well, thanks. See you around."

She stepped back into the nest of discarded packaging and open potting soil bags. "Thanks for coming by with that. I'll pay more attention next time."

"It was no problem. Are you sure you don't want help with those rocks?"

Part of her desperately wanted to say yes. And not just the muscles in her back that were already aching in anticipation of the shoveling. She wanted to say yes... because she enjoyed his company? That couldn't be right.

"I'm good. Thanks anyway."

Ross shrugged. "Suit yourself. Bye Andrea." He turned toward his car after flashing that crooked grin again.

She narrowed her eyes and watched him walk away. Good riddance.

Still, she bit the inside of her cheek to keep the smile from growing. Ross was certainly persistent. If she wasn't moving home in three weeks, maybe they could be friends.

4

The drive from Virginia to Western Indiana took most of a day, and when Andi pulled off the highway onto the wide gravel road that led to Bloom's Farm, the sun was dipping below the horizon. If she had a passenger, the growl of her stomach could probably be heard over the podcast playing. Despite the temptation of the fast-food restaurants along the interstate, Andi kept driving. Nothing would beat the food at home and the welcome reception waiting for her.

The gravel road curved gently, and the rustic sign welcoming her to Bloom's Farm stretched across the small gravel driveway. Her smile broadening at the sight.

She exhaled deeply, a previously unnoticed weight lifting from her shoulders.

Home.

Slowing the car to a stop, she snapped a photo and texted it to Monique and Sarah.

AB: Made it home.

Then she pulled through the open gate, eagerly following the gravel drive toward the place she'd always called home. On the right stood Storybook Barn, the event venue run by her sister Lily. A bit farther and she passed the bed-and-breakfast run by Daisy. When the road forked, she took the right-hand drive toward the big house.

The number of cars shouldn't have surprised her. The circle drive and the grassy yard were filled with trucks, minivans, and cars. Between her six siblings— and their spouses—any family get-together needed its own parking lot these days.

She parked and grabbed the half-empty Dr Pepper from the cup holder along with her purse. Andi had stepped one leg out before she heard the shriek from the front porch. Daisy ran toward her at full speed. "You're here! You're really here!"

Andi laughed and shut the door just in time to be wrapped in a hug. Her sister's arms squeezed tightly around her. "Oh my goodness, it's so good to see you."

"It hasn't been that long." Andi had been home six months ago for Christmas.

"I know, but now you're really here. And you're not leaving this time." Daisy stepped back. "Right? You're not leaving?"

Andi shook her head. "Nope. You're stuck with me."

"Are you staying at the house? Do you need a room at the bed-and-breakfast? Will you get an apartment in town?" In true Daisy fashion, the questions came fast and furious with no time to respond. "Never mind, you can tell me later. Everyone is inside waiting for you!"

Daisy pulled her arm and Andi allowed herself to be led inside.

The house smelled like garlic and basil, a sure sign that her mom had fixed something special.

"She's here!"

"Who?" Hawthorne's clueless tone was matched with a mischievous grin. "Are we expecting someone?"

Andi chuckled, and her older brother wrapped her in a hug. "Good to see you. Welcome home."

Round the room she went, engulfed in warm

hugs from her sisters and awkward embraces from the brothers-in-law she barely knew. Sure, she knew Lily's husband Josh pretty well. Other than that, she knew Lance best—both since he'd been around the longest and because she video chatted with Daisy at least once a week.

Her mother was in the kitchen, pulling garlic bread out of the oven. "Perfect timing, Andi. Dinner is just about done. I'm so glad you're home." She pulled off her oven mitts and set them on the counter before opening her arms wide. Andi tucked herself into them willingly.

"Come on, come on. What's an old man got to do to get a hug from his daughter?"

Her mom released her and a smile spread across her face. "Dad!"

Keith Bloom stood on the other side of the kitchen with a huge smile. "Dandelion."

Andi resisted the urge to roll her eyes. Her parents were the only ones who ever called her by her full name. Enveloped in her dad's arms, Andi sighed. This was home. A lot had changed over the years—there were way more men around the room, for one thing. Her parents seemed markedly older every time she came home. Her dad had recovered from the stroke he'd suffered eight years ago, but his hug would never have the strength she remembered.

Little faces greeted her from every corner. Older ones were parked in front of a movie in the living room, and the younger ones clung to her sisters— their mothers. Daisy's daughter, Brielle, finally noticed she was there and ran to hug her. They'd been to visit her a few times, so Brielle knew her better than most of the others. She was looking forward to being Aunt Andi around the farm from here on out.

"It's so good to be home."

Dinner kicked off with a prayer from her father before devolving into the organized chaos that was to be expected with a gathering of nearly twenty people.

Lily leaned over and cut the meatball on her daughter's plate. "How was the drive, Andi?"

"It was long. A little traffic in Columbus, but otherwise it was pretty much open roads." She searched the room and finally located Lavender at the other end of the table. "I listened to your new book, Lovey!"

Lavender smiled shyly. "You didn't have to do that."

"Of course I did. You're my sister. I still can't believe you are a published author."

"Hey, what about me?" Lavender's husband, Emmett, pretended to be offended from his place at the counter, where he was dishing a second helping.

Andi waved a hand. "Yeah, yeah. Reclusive best-selling author. We know." She winked to let him know she was joking. Andi had read all of his books, as well.

"New York Times *number one* bestselling author," Lavender clarified, her voice filled with pride.

"What? Seriously, dude?" Lily's husband, and Emmett's best friend, Josh, jumped in. "I didn't know that. When did that happen?"

"Last week," Emmett said with a shrug. "It's no big deal."

"It's a very big deal, Em. Way to go." Josh clapped a heavy hand on Emmett's shoulder. His tattoo peeked out from under the short sleeve of his shirt. Andi wasn't phased by a man with tattoos—how could she be in the Army? But it still made her smile that her perfectly proper sister Lily had ended up with the muscle-bound, motorcycle-riding photographer.

"That's awesome, Emmett," she agreed. "Was it

The Firecaster of Arkyndia? I loved that book. I think I read it twice the first week it came out."

Emmett's eyes grew wide. "You read my books?"

Andi raised an eyebrow. "Yeah?" She looked around. "You guys don't think I keep track of you?" She looked around the room. "Josh had a big gallery show last month in Chicago. I bought one of the photos, even though I was in Baltimore." She saw her sister-in-law, a chemical engineering professor. "Avery presented a big paper at the Sustainable Energy Summit this summer. It went way over my head, but I watched the live stream." She shrugged. "Rumor has it Harrison is on the short list for Vice President, partially due to the record low unemployment he's sustained in Indiana and partially because women under the age of fifty go crazy for him, at least according to the polls."

Harrison buried his face in his hands and laughter rang out around the table.

"You really keep track of all that?"

Andi nodded. "I have news alerts set up on all of you. I figure even if I talk to Daisy every day, there is something she's bound to forget—no matter how much she likes to share everyone else's news." She smiled indulgently at her twin.

Daisy shrugged. "Guilty as charged. Even I

didn't know about Avery's paper or Harrison's poll numbers though."

"Actually, about that..." Harrison's voice rose above the chatter. "We have an announcement." He stood next to Poppy and they joined hands. Andi remembered the turmoil of their relationship's rocky start, and she was so happy to see the love that had blossomed between her sister and the current Governor of Indiana. They'd gone to high school together, and when Harrison had wanted to become the governor, he turned to Poppy for help. Since then, he'd made the journey from local senate representative to state governor.

The family quieted and Harrison looked at Poppy. "I met with Senator Waters this week, and she asked me if I would accept a position as her official running mate." Andi's eyes widened. When her brother-in-law's name was being thrown around as a candidate for Vice President, the idea had still seemed abstract. But Senator Waters had just been named the official candidate and was ahead of the opposing party's candidate by a healthy margin. She was going to be the first woman president.

"Poppy and I had already been praying about it. And today, I called her back to accept."

Whoa. That was huge. Andi clapped and cheered along with everyone else.

"How exciting!"

"Congratulations!"

Harrison shook hands with her brothers-in-law and accepted hugs from everyone else.

Andi gave him a hug. "You'll have my vote, Harrison."

"Thanks, Andi. I'm really glad you're home, and actually we will have some things to talk about."

She gave a confused look, and he continued. "I plan to have my campaign headquarters in Indianapolis, but I'll host quite a few events and special guests here at the farm during the campaign."

Andi nodded. "Got it. Security. Yeah, no problem. I've got you covered."

He flashed the pearly white smile that had taken him from Indiana's most eligible bachelor list to the governor's mansion, and now—the White House. "Thanks. I know between you and the Secret Service, we'll be in good hands."

Andi frowned at the realization that she would barely have time to settle in as head of security before another team invaded and tried to take over. Well, whoever the Secret Service assigned better recognize that she wasn't some two-bit security guard.

First thing tomorrow, she'd start a full-scale review of the farm's security measures and make sure there were no holes for the suits to find.

Her mom clapped her hands and raised her voice to be heard. "What an amazing opportunity, Harrison. I think this is cause for celebration!"

Andi called out, "Hey now, I thought I was the cause for celebration?"

Her mom wagged a finger at her. "Oh, hush. Of course. We are celebrating both things tonight!"

"How about one more thing to celebrate?" Lavender always amazed Andi in the way she could command a room with her quiet, confident tone. Andi always felt like she needed to be stern and formidable to get the message across.

"Of course, Lovey! What is it?"

She took Emmett's hand. "Well, Caleb is going to be a big brother! We're pregnant with twins."

Andi felt the moisture gather in her eyes at the obviously emotional announcement from her sister. Andi had never wanted children of her own, but she was thrilled for Lavender and Emmett. They'd walked a tough road of infertility for a couple of years before Caleb was born. He'd just turned one.

Lily and Josh had faced infertility as well, but even treatments would have been risky, and they eventually decided it was safer to adopt. Andi glanced at Maia, the sassy four-year-old currently rubbing Lavender's belly as though she could already see the babies inside.

"Oh my... Twins?" Their mom was sobbing now, making her way across the dining room to take Lavender in her arms.

This was something she was especially grateful to be home for. She'd witnessed countless announcements of engagements, pregnancies, or new jobs while she was alone in her condo, watching through a screen. And if the tears on her face were any indication, it was a big difference to be there in person. She swiped at the tears stealthily. Andi wasn't a crier.

She'd prayed for Lavender and Emmett's journey for years. To witness them announcing another pregnancy without all the fertility treatments they needed last time was a huge blessing.

Cool Aunt Andi would have two more kids to spoil. Last summer during a visit, Avery and Andi had bonded over their feelings about kids. They both loved them—and loved sending them home to their parents.

Twins, eh? She glanced at Daisy. "She has no idea what she's in for with twins."

Daisy grinned. "Not at all."

Another round of hugs all around, and finally dessert was served.

"I'd like to pray," her father said. The room quieted, and he began. "Father, Your Word says there is a time to rejoice. And I can't help but imagine the author meant exactly a time like this. Our blessings are overflowing abundantly, Lord. We are so grateful. Please never let us forget that all these good things come from you. Thank You for bringing Andi home. Thank You for blessing Harrison's career. Please continue to give him wisdom as the lion's den he is entering will only grow fiercer. And thank You for the beautiful gift of life within Lavender right now. Knit them together perfectly in your image. Just..." He choked on the emotion and Andi felt her own throat sting. "Thank you for letting me be here to witness all of this."

Andi couldn't agree more.

She was home.

At last.

5

*R*oss scanned the crowd, looking for anything out of the ordinary. Any suspicious movements, any angry facial expressions in a crowd that should only be bored at worst was an indicator to look deeper. His earpiece clicked on and the team leader's voice came over the radio.

"Position one, check in."

Ross's eyes found the agent across the ballroom at the north entrance and watched him respond at the same time he heard the response via his earpiece. "All clear."

"Position two?"

"Nothing but a bunch of rich dudes."

Ross didn't wait for the team lead to jump in. "Claussen." His voice held a hint of warning.

"Position Two. All clear," Claussen said with a sigh.

Ross felt his jaw tighten. He was going to have a chat with him later. If this job wasn't exciting enough for Claussen, he was in the wrong field. Exciting days on protection detail meant someone was either getting hurt or trying to hurt someone. Those were not good days.

Status updates continued to register in his ear as he surveyed the space. There were no anticipated problems at this relatively low-key, high-dollar fundraiser, but he knew he wouldn't relax until he was in his hotel room tonight and had kicked off his specially made dress shoes. Tomorrow, his team would be on a flight home.

A longer assignment was only a matter of time. Senator Waters had officially been named the candidate running against the current president. She'd announce her running mate any day, and Ross had already been told he was slated for the team lead on the VP candidate's personal detail. It would be his biggest role ever, and he wasn't going to screw it up.

A flash of movement to his right made him turn his head, and Ross immediately zeroed in on the angry expression of a man pushing through the crowd.

He set his path on an intersection with the angry man's march and spoke quietly into his earpiece. "Suspicious white male, black jacket, moving toward position two. Moving to intersect."

"I see him."

"I think I saw him arguing with a woman in the hallway," Ross heard Claussen say.

He relaxed a bit but continued watching the man carefully. A lover's quarrel? It could make someone march across the room in an upset hurry, but was that all this was?

The man's eyes were focused ahead, and Ross followed his gaze. Senator Waters stood twenty feet ahead in a small circle of Florida's most generous donors.

Ross was closing in. Ten feet from the senator, he grabbed the man by the shoulders and walked him toward a nearby exit.

"Senator!" The man yelled at Waters while struggling slightly against Ross's strength. "Senator!"

There were a few interested looks from the group around the senator, but Ross took the man into the hallway, with one arm wrenched behind his back.

"Are there others?" He hissed in the man's ear.

He shook his head in response and Ross tightened the arm hold. "Are. There. Others?"

The man cried out, "No! It's just me." A sob escaped. "It's just me."

Ross loosened his grip. "Suspect in custody. Be on the lookout for accomplices. But I think he's alone."

Rogers barreled down the hallway toward them.

"I just wanted to talk to her!" The suspect's pleas were desperate and pitiful.

Ross frowned. "You didn't look like you were gearing up for a conversation. We are pretty good at reading people, and you looked like you wanted to punch her lights out."

"It's all her fault! I need to tell her!"

Rogers grabbed the man's arm. "Write a letter next time. Come on, let's go. You're coming with us."

The next day, Ross slipped off his black shoes and dress socks and set them at the edge of the sand where the wooden sidewalk ended. This was ridiculous, but Rogers had wanted to see the beach. He stepped onto the sand, then paused to roll up his pant legs. He probably looked about as out of place as a sail boat in the desert, with his black suit and tie on the beach.

"Come on, McClain. We've only got a half hour before we need to head to the airport."

And that was why the suit would be staying on.

Florida was supposed to be an easy trip. In and out for a simple event, only needed for the day of. Which meant Ross had been up most of the night writing his report about what had happened at the dinner and why it ended with him quietly escorting an angry man out of the event. He still had a few more things to bring up with his boss when they got back to DC.

Something about last night didn't sit right with him. On the surface, it seemed totally normal. The man had paid for a ticket to the event and passed all the background checks. But he couldn't help feel a nagging similarity to what had happened in Denver. Ross's stomach twisted at the thought of a leak. He cared about his fellow agents like brothers.

Should he bring up his suspicions to Agent Gallo? If he was right, then someone would be in serious trouble. If he were wrong, casting shadows on an innocent man wouldn't look good at all.

Of course, missing their flight because Rogers needed to stick his toes in the sand wouldn't look good to anyone. He checked his watch for the fifteenth time since they pulled into the parking lot. They were fine. Plenty of time.

He made it five more minutes before calling it. Ross let out a loud whistle and waved a finger in the air—the international symbol for 'wrap it up.' Before climbing into the car, Ross gently unrolled his pant legs, frowning at the sand that fell out despite his precautions.

He was ready to be home. Maybe he could make it to the dojo tonight after the flight landed. Maybe Andi would even be there. Which shouldn't even matter, since she had dismissed him so easily at her house.

He shook off the way her dismissal rankled. He didn't need to be liked. "Let's go, guys. We've got a plane to catch."

ANDI LOOKED around the small office next to Lily's attached to Storybook Barn. It was smaller than her closet at the condo, and that was saying something.

The room featured one tiny window and a shabby desk. A lonely computer monitor sat on the desk, with enough dust on the screen to inspire whomever had been here last to draw a smiley face in it with their finger.

"This is it?"

Lily shrugged. "We don't use it much."

Andi raised an eyebrow. "Do we use it at all?"

"Last year there was a fight in the parking lot and the police asked for a copy of the tape. That was the last time I even looked at it."

Andi sighed. "Okay, tell me what you've got."

"The camera in the parking lot was more for peace of mind, so no one broke into cars during a reception or something. It's on a motion sensor. Saves any footage in this computer and starts overwriting the oldest footage when the drive is full."

Andi tried not to let her dismay show. "How big is the drive?"

"I don't know. I think it usually holds about a week?"

"So that's it? That's the extent of security for the whole farm?"

"You might ask Hawthorne to be sure, but yeah. Maybe Daisy has something separate at the inn? And I think Rose had some cameras set up around the pastures, but I don't know if Lindsay kept them or not." Andi hadn't met the new livestock and petting zoo manager yet, but everyone spoke highly of the young woman from Minden.

Andi jiggled the mouse and the computer came to life. The login screen blinked at her. That was a pleasant surprise. "Password?"

"Storybook barn, one word," her sister replied.

Of course it was. She logged in to make sure it worked. "Okay, thanks."

When she scooted the chair back to sit down, it nearly hit the wall behind her. Lily laughed. "There's another office on the other side of this wall. Maybe I made them a little too small."

Andi raised an eyebrow. "You think?"

"In my defense, they were just supposed to be storage closets."

"Noted. Any reason I couldn't combine them into one room?"

"Not that I know of. Maybe check with Hawthorne first?"

"Will do. I need to touch base with him anyway."

"Do you have a radio yet?" When Andi shook her head, Lily extended her handheld walkie-talkie. "You can borrow mine. I rarely use it unless there is an event going on."

"Thanks."

Andi called for Hawthorne and arranged to meet him at the bed-and-breakfast. She was already headed that way to check in with Daisy. The heat of the day was starting to creep in, but Andi wasn't complaining, even in her long black cargo pants. Once you'd spent a week in the desert before the air conditioners had arrived... An Indiana August wasn't going to phase her.

She strolled across the field that spread from Storybook Barn toward the bed-and-breakfast. It had recently been baled, and the round bales dotted the landscape. Lily had convinced Hawthorne that the field between the gate and the event barn needed regular mowing, but here on the backside of the hill was the reminder that this was still a working farm. Besides, Andi had seen enough wedding photos that featured cowboy hats and hay bales to know that the rural Indiana clientele didn't mind the farm aesthetic.

She jogged up the steps of Bloom's Farm Bed and Breakfast. The old homestead had seen a huge transformation when Daisy tackled the idea of turning it into an inn. The white trim and green siding were cute and homey.

Andi knocked lightly before opening the door. Straight ahead down the hall, Daisy poked her head out of the dining room. "I'll be just a minute. Why don't you sit in the kitchen and keep Bonnie company?"

She headed into the kitchen and was welcomed into a hug by the elderly homemaker who served breakfast each morning. "Come in, come in. Your sister is clearing the table," Bonnie Mae gave her a grin, "and cleaning up the pitcher of orange juice she spilled when Mr. Matthews walked in."

A smile tugged at her lips. Somewhere along the way, her graceful dancer sister had turned into a klutz because of the presence of her contractor-turned-husband. "Sounds sticky," she commented.

Bonnie laughed, a full-bellied sound that bounced around the kitchen with its gleaming stainless-steel appliances. "You hungry, sugar?"

"Always," Andi confirmed. Whatever cinnamon concoction was making the kitchen smell so good was sure to require an extra mile tonight, but Andi liked running the country roads anyway.

Bonnie set a plate in front of her with a slice of quiche and a cinnamon roll, oozing with frosting and the brown cinnamon filling. Andi's mouth watered instantly.

"Coffee?"

"No thanks. Never liked the stuff." She'd drunk it out of desperation a time or two, until she'd discovered caffeine pills. All the kick, none of the bitterness.

"Don't tell me you drink Dr Pepper for breakfast like that sister of yours."

Andi laughed. "No, not for me." At least not for breakfast. She tried to stick with tea or water, but occasionally, the call of the sugary drink was too strong to resist. "Do you have tea?"

Bonnie brought her a mug of hot water from the carafe. Andi was two bites into the cinnamon roll when Daisy came in, blowing her bangs out of her face with a laugh. "Remind me to buy pitchers with a lid next time." She set a stack of dirty dishes on the counter, then threw a handful of dirty rags into a container by the door. "Morning, Andi. Is Bonnie taking good care of you?"

She gave a moan of pleasure. "Can I move in here? This is incredible."

Bonnie blushed. "Come on by anytime."

"Don't listen to her, Andi. She'd be feeding the entire staff every day if I didn't rescind the invitations she so freely hands out." Daisy went back through the doors to the dining room.

Bonnie whispered. "What she doesn't know won't hurt her. Hawthorne stops by about once a week while Daisy is stripping beds. And Josh sneaks breakfast every time he has a wedding on-site. So you just come by when you need a pick me up, all right?"

Andi nodded and hid her smile behind her mug when Daisy came back in.

"So, what did you need from me, Andi? I haven't really thought too much about security around the bed-and-breakfast."

"Do you have any sort of system in place?"

Daisy shook her head. "No? I mean, we have key cards for the doors to the rooms. But that's about it."

Andi nodded. Keycards were a good start. "Have you ever had any trouble? Unwelcome visitors, break-ins?"

Daisy rolled her eyes. "Come on. This is Rogers County, this isn't DC. The closest thing to trouble we see is a fight between a couple who is supposed to be on their second honeymoon."

"How does that get handled?"

Daisy shifted her weight and looked out the window. "I don't know. Whatever makes sense at the time. I call Lance or Hawthorne. Or the police." Andi saw her sister getting defensive and agitated.

"Whoa, whoa. Don't worry, Daze. You've been doing awesome. I'm just trying to anticipate what might be needed around here. Wouldn't it be nice for your night staff to know what to do? To have someone specific to call?"

"Yeah, I guess it would."

"Okay. I really think we should have a full-house security system for this place. There's a lot of traffic on the main drive between festivals and the petting zoo and weddings. Access should really be restricted to guests."

"Yeah, that's true. I have actually found more than one lost wedding guest who decided our sitting room was a good place to take a nap."

Andi winced. "See? Especially when there are times we leave the house unattended, except for guests, the house should be secured. Don't worry—it won't be intrusive or distracting. What is the software you use for the door locks?"

After she had written down the information from Daisy, Andi tucked back into her breakfast. Daisy went to check out the guests. Hawthorne stepped through the front door, holding it open for a man struggling with two suitcases and a duffle bag. He met her eye and raised a finger. "I'll be right back."

Andi watched out the window as Hawthorne offered a hand to the man and helped him load the suitcases into his car. She smiled. Hawthorne had certainly matured since she lived here last. It was nice to see him willing to help.

He jogged back inside and entered the kitchen, taking a deep inhale. "I can't thank you enough for setting this meeting here. Morning, Bonnie." He kissed the older woman on the cheek and she swatted him with a dish towel.

"Go sit down, charmer. I'll fix you a plate."

Hawthorne patted his stomach. "Daisy says I can't eat here every day. Probably a good thing." Andi scoffed. Hawthorne might be getting older, but he was a far cry from a pot-bellied middle-aged man. All the work on the farm made sure of that.

Daisy rolled her eyes when she came back in and saw Hawthorne eating at the small kitchen table. Andi bit her lip to keep from laughing.

"Okay, okay. We are here to do actual work, not just eat Bonnie Mae's delicious food. So let's chat."

Hawthorne nodded but shoveled another bite of cinnamon roll into his mouth. "I'm all ears," he said with a full mouth.

Andi narrowed her eyes. Typical Hawthorne. Apparently, Avery hadn't smoothed all his rough edges. "I want to talk vision here. You brought me on board, and I want to know why. Is this just a pity thing? A ploy to get me to come home? Because I can find another job." She was meeting later tonight with a realtor to look at gym space to open a dojo in Terre Haute. She could do more than just security at the farm. A dojo made sense. She didn't have any other ideas anyway.

Hawthorne shook his head and swallowed. "Not a chance. Look, Andi—I brought you on because I've been thinking we need a security person for a while now. Are you overqualified? Probably. But you're also family, which means I can trust you completely."

She relaxed. That made sense. Still, Andi didn't know what Hawthorne expected. She knew what she would do, but was it in line with her brother—or rather, her new boss?

"What do you see as the needs for security then?"

Hawthorne gestured to the surrounding room. "We've got to get this place taken care of. This and Storybook are our biggest concerns in my opinion. The animals and the crops, not so much. The main house would be good too. Mom and Dad are there alone a lot—or at least, they were until you moved back."

Andi nodded. She wouldn't be living there forever. Hopefully. It made sense to wrap the main house into the security system for the farm. "Okay. I've got some ideas, but I need a rough idea of the budget. It's going to take some investment to get things implemented."

"I get that. I'll send you the numbers for what we can swing. But we need to talk to Harrison too. This whole thing changes when we consider the added needs of his events."

Right. Harrison Coulter, candidate for vice president. She considered what that would look like. "We'll need security at their house, and we might as well tie it into our system. Technically, that's not Bloom's Farm property, but we'll work out the details. Send him a bill or whatever. He'll have a Secret Service detail. Probably a small one, but still. We'll need to factor that in."

Hawthorne nodded. "Don't do anything too extreme just because of his stuff, but that's definitely one reason we need to get our house in order sooner rather than later."

"Understood."

That night, Andi met the realtor in front of an empty strip mall location in Terre Haute. Crammed in the space between a sandwich shop and a hair salon, the broken sign for a long-closed insurance office hung above a dirty window.

Andi tried to let her imagination take over. She should have brought Daisy along. How her sister had been able to look at the old house and see the potential was amazing. Andi apparently did not share her sister's vision for that kind of thing. Because right now, she couldn't see this rundown storefront operating as a dojo.

"This is a great location," the realtor was saying. But Andi was peering through the glass, looking for a glimpse of what lay inside.

When the real estate agent finally took her inside, Andi's reservations grew. There were walls that would need taken out. And the ceilings were low. She tried to picture what it would look like with gym mats and a row of kids dressed in white martial arts uniforms.

Something didn't feel right, so she thanked the real estate agent and said goodbye.

It seemed like opening a dojo should be the perfect thing for her. She could help on the farm as needed, teach students the art she loved, and also help women by offering self-defense classes.

Yet, when she began to think about the steps moving forward with the plan, she got an uneasy feeling in her stomach. She'd had that feeling before —usually in combat, and usually before something bad happened. Was this God's way of telling her to wait? Or not to do it at all?

She wasn't sure, but she knew that she wouldn't move forward when it didn't feel like the right thing. She had to trust that God would make it obvious what the right move was, or at least what the right move was not.

6

*R*oss stepped off the airplane in Indianapolis and made his way to the rental car center. For the next six months, he was technically a part of the Indianapolis field office. He'd still report to Gallo, since he was the special agent in charge of the Vice Presidential Candidate Protective Task Force. Their office, the Special Operations Division, was the protective division in charge of nonpermanent protection for U.S. Citizens. Like Indiana Governor Harrison Coulter, apparently.

Governor Coulter had just been announced as the vice presidential candidate and was therefore officially granted Secret Service protection. Ross didn't know much about the man, but he seemed nice enough. From the initial consult with the governor here in Indianapolis last week, he learned they would split their time between Indianapolis, some place called Bloom's Farm, and wherever else on the campaign trail they were needed.

The rest of his team would arrive later this week. Today Ross was driving to Bloom's Farm to figure out exactly what that particular unknown held. He wasn't expecting much. It wouldn't be hard to protect a house and some land. Probably easier than the rest of the detail, which would include accompanying Governor Coulter in hotels, offices, airports, and worst of all—campaign stops with unpredictable crowds and lots of handshakes and selfies.

He'd surveyed the Indianapolis residence while he was here last week, but as the Governor's Mansion, it already had security in place, and his team would simply be added. Same for his office at the capitol.

The drive to Bloom's Farm was peaceful. The flat, open landscape reminded Ross of home in Iowa. He should be close enough to swing a visit, probably sometime when Coulter had a weekend off and was spending it at this farm place. The discovery of a Bloom's Farm Bed and Breakfast had been a welcome surprise. Ross had booked himself a room for the next few days until his team arrived. Then they'd need to find somewhere larger to stay.

When the GPS directed him off the highway and onto a narrower country road, Ross turned the music down and focused on finding the turnoff. A flash of neon on the side of the road made him slow even further in the dim twilight. He moved his car over to give the runner space on the edge of the road. She was fit—and fast. Wait a second, was that…?

Okay, now he was imagining things. He hadn't seen Andi since their paint exchange nearly a month ago. Every time he'd been back in town, he'd gone to the dojo. Definitely not trying to run into her, but he wouldn't have minded a chance to practice with her again. He'd mentally relived that particular match a hundred times while running through his katas in hotel rooms. And the lively banter that had gone with it.

Now he was seeing Andi in Middle of Nowhere, Indiana? He shook his head and moved the car back over to his lane and watched the runner disappear in his rearview mirror. He needed to focus on the job. And he definitely needed to find Bloom's Farm before it got dark, or he'd be sleeping in his rental car.

His GPS didn't fail him though, and the voice announced his arrival just as he spotted the large rustic sign stretching over a gravel driveway. He followed the drive like the bed-and-breakfast website had instructed him. A barn sat in a field to his right, and the sign proclaiming Bloom's Farm Bed and Breakfast sat in front of a large house, nestled in a bed of landscaping and lit with soft spotlights.

Ross parked the nondescript gray sedan and climbed out and went to the back of the car to grab his bag.

"Mr. McClain?" Ross turned toward the voice. When he saw the speaker, his suitcase slipped from his grasp and landed with a *thunk*—directly on his toe.

He bit back a swear word, then looked back up. "Andi?"

There was a look of surprise on the woman's face. Then he realized it couldn't be Andi. This woman had much longer hair. Her face wore a casual smile instead of the seemingly permanent scowl of his sparring partner. He raised a hand to interrupt her. "Sorry, I thought you were someone else."

Her eyes danced with laughter. "It's okay. I'm Daisy. Welcome to Bloom's Farm, Mr. McClain."

She showed him inside and checked him in. Daisy was talkative enough and Ross was happy to let her talk.

"Come on in. Have you ever stayed here before?" She didn't wait for an answer. "My husband and I renovated this house a few years back. It's my favorite place in the whole world." She gave a quick tour. "Here's the sitting room. You're welcome to hang out anywhere in the house. The sunroom in the back is especially nice in the early evenings." She paused. "What brings you to the area, Mr. McClain?"

"I'm here on business. Do you know Governor Coulter?" Judging by her personality, Daisy probably knew everyone in a three-county radius.

Daisy laughed. "Harrison? Of course I do. You're clearly not from around here. Harrison is married to my sister, Poppy."

Ross nodded. Now he was tracking with the dossier he'd received on Coulter. Married to Poppy Bloom. Bloom's Farm.

"So are you in politics? Or are you a lawyer?"

It was his turn to laugh. "Neither. I'll be leading the governor's security detail for the duration of the campaign."

Daisy's eyes widened. When her smile disappeared, she looked so much like Andi it was kind of freaking him out. "You're his bodyguard?"

Ross tried not to bristle at the label. An agent

was so much more than a bodyguard. He'd spent years in a field office doing investigative work and protective details before moving into the Special Operations Division. He was responsible for so much more than just standing next to someone and looking tough. Still, she wasn't trying to be offensive. "It's a little more than that."

"That's so cool. I can't believe we have a Secret Service agent staying here. Here," she reached for his bag, "let me show you to your room."

He waved off her hand and carried his bag up the stairs. After Daisy left him alone, Ross sat on the bed. Tomorrow he had appointments with Governor Coulter and the head of security for this place. Ross grabbed his phone. Apparently, his preconceived notions about Bloom's Farm were a little off. From what Daisy had said during her rambling, this was more like a regional tourist attraction than a personal residence.

He flipped through the website. Weddings, festivals, even a petting zoo? Governor Coulter had to be kidding. Living here during the campaign meant thousands of unvetted individuals on site each month.

Ross laid back on the bed and groaned softly. He said a prayer for wisdom and patience. Then he sat up and pulled out a notebook to jot down questions to ask the governor tomorrow. And a separate list for the head of security. What was his name? He pulled up the email from Rogers.

I spoke to the manager at Bloom's Farm. You have an appointment with the head of security (Andy) at Storybook Barn on Thursday at 1:00 p.m.

Hopefully Andy knew what he was doing, or at least admitted that he didn't. Ross knew that dropping a protective detail into the middle of an existing operation could go a couple of ways. In his experience, it worked out better for everyone if the local guys allowed his team to take the lead and do their jobs. If they could follow orders, everything would work out fine.

In the morning, Ross quickly decided he was never leaving the bed-and-breakfast. The rest of his team could stay in Terre Haute, but he should probably stay on site full-time, right? At least, that was what the eggs Benedict was trying to convince him of.

"Agent McClain, good morning." Daisy greeted him warmly, then smiled sheepishly. "My sister informed me I should call you agent instead of mister."

He smiled. "Your sister is technically correct." He would say that it didn't bother him, but that would be a lie and he didn't like to lie. He had worked his tail off to become a special agent for the Secret Service. Plus it helped him maintain a separation from the job for people to refer to him as an agent instead of his first name. Especially on longer assignments, it was easy to get too close to the people around the protectee. In whatever scenario, his job was to protect his assigned person—not their sister. In some cases, even their kids were excluded. Which meant it was risky to get too close.

"How's breakfast? Can I get you anything?"

"It's delicious."

Daisy smiled broadly. "Bonnie Mae is the best, isn't she?"

Ross had to agree. The elderly woman had doted on him since he stepped into the dining room. Another reason he was seriously considering staying here, instead of at the chain hotel in Terre Haute that would be serving powdered eggs and rubbery sausage.

He checked his watch and finished his coffee. He was supposed to meet with Governor Coulter this morning at some place called Storybook Barn.

"Excuse me, Mrs. Matthews? What is the best way to get to Storybook Barn?"

"Right this way. I'll show you." She led him out the front door and onto the porch. Then Daisy extended her finger straight ahead. "That is Storybook Barn."

In the light of the morning, he could see the large wooden barn was a dark gray brown. It was rustic, but meticulously updated and maintained.

"Well, okay then. I suppose I won't get lost on my way there."

Daisy laughed. "You're funny too? This should be interesting."

Ross furrowed his brow. What was she talking about? "Huh?"

Daisy waved a hand. "Oh, nothing. Let me know if you need anything else. I'll be here all day."

"Thanks."

Ross climbed into his car to make a few phone calls with the privacy it afforded. Daisy seemed like the type who wouldn't intentionally try to eavesdrop, but who wouldn't walk away from the chance to hear a conversation she wasn't supposed to.

"Gallo."

"Hey, boss. I'm on-site. Headed to a meeting with Coulter here in a few minutes."

"Good. What's your first thought?"

"His rural residence is a bit more complicated than we thought. This place is more like a business than a farm. I'm still trying to get the lay of the land, but tell the team to do a web search to see what we're dealing with. I'll update later after the meetings."

"All right. Rogers and Claussen are just wrapping up the advance work for the stops in Quad Cities, Des Moines and Omaha next week."

"Roger that."

Ross walked to the barn, since the morning was clear and it wasn't far. It was a nice change of pace from the cities he usually worked in. A large dirty truck ambled toward him down the driveway, slowing when it pulled alongside him with the passenger window already down.

"Beautiful morning, isn't it?" The man wore a baseball cap and a broad smile that Ross couldn't help but return. He didn't seem at all concerned about the stranger walking down the drive, which was slightly concerning since Ross was here to check out the security gaps and protocols.

"It sure is."

"I'm TJ. I manage the produce operation here. You need anything?"

Ross shook his head. "Nice to meet you, TJ. I'm just headed up to Storybook Barn for a meeting."

"Well then, I won't keep you. Lily can be a real stickler about things. I've never met anyone more organized."

Ross filed away the information, even though he wasn't meeting with Lily—whoever that was. She sounded like the polar opposite of Daisy, who had fumbled to find the reservation book last night and misplaced her water bottle three times during breakfast. Daisy and Lily? Oh, and Poppy. What was with all the flower names around here?

TJ continued driving toward the rest of the farm and left Ross to finish the short walk to the barn. The gravel parking lot was fairly large, and the field showed some evidence that parking on the grass wasn't unheard of. The barn had a large patio on one side, and there were flowers and even a fountain within the landscaped beds around the entrance.

The towering wooden door was propped open with a large rock and Ross knocked before opening it and peeking his head in.

"Hello?"

It took a moment for his eyes to adjust. Compared to the bright sun, the interior of the barn was dark, despite the windows letting in shafts of light.

A sharply dressed woman emerged from a doorway on the left. She smiled warmly. "You must be Agent McClain. Harrison told me you were meeting here this morning."

"I'm going to guess you are Lily?"

"Good guess. I manage all the weddings and events that are hosted at Storybook Barn."

He stuck out his hand. "Nice to meet you."

"Aunt Lily!" The high-pitched squeal made him jump and turn, just in time to see the long brown hair of a young girl run past him and into Lily's arms.

A deep voice with an amused tone called out, "Magnolia, try to keep the volume down while we are inside, please."

Ross turned back toward the door. He'd met Governor Coulter last week, but he looked quite different this morning. Instead of the suit from their meeting at the capitol building, the governor wore jeans and a tucked-in polo. An appraising glance at the man's shoes revealed a pair of boots with a covering of creases and dust that couldn't be faked. Ross had learned long ago that a man's shoes didn't lie. Harrison Coulter was every bit a country boy as he claimed in his campaign commercials. A loose smile covered the governor's face as he strolled toward Ross with an outstretched hand.

"Agent McClain, it's good to see you again. Please excuse my daughter. This is Magnolia. She begged me to bring her with me." Coulter turned to Lily and said, "I told her she had to help you with whatever you need. So put her to work, Lil."

Lily laid a hand on the young girl's head. "I think we've got some napkins to fold. You ready to be a big helper?" At Magnolia's excited response, Lily looked back up. "I'll leave you two to talk. Let me know if you need anything. We'll be in the laundry room."

Ross watched Lily and Magnolia disappear through the door before turning back to Coulter.

"Any trouble finding the place?"

"Nope, GPS knew right where to find it."

"Glad to hear it. Daisy said you stayed at the bed-and-breakfast last night?"

Ross's lips twitched. Daisy had mentioned talking to her sister, but apparently that also extended to her brother-in-law. "I did. I met Bonnie Mae and I'm trying to convince her to marry me."

Coulter laughed. "Understandable. You're not the first to try, I'll tell you that."

"Do you want to sit and talk through things, or did you have another plan?"

"Let's sit. I'll let the locals show you around the farm later."

They pulled a couple of chairs from the closet and sat at one of the large round tables in the open space. Ross took several pages of notes as the governor explained his plans for time here at home. From what Ross heard, this location would be a combination of where Coulter would be during down-time and a place where he hosted a few larger events like fundraisers and the election night party.

"You remember Neil Powers, my political advisor?" Ross nodded. The man had been at the meeting last week. "He thinks this would be a good place to host a few key donors for some personal visits."

Ross nodded and made a note. "Do you have a list of those people yet?"

Coulter shook his head. "I'm afraid that's not my expertise. I'm sure Neil is already putting one together. I'll have him send it to you."

"Sounds good. We'll have to run background checks on them and have a little bit of advance notice, but small visits like that are easy enough. The larger events though, that's trickier. We will need to bring in extra agents from the Indianapolis field office, as well as local law enforcement."

Harrison nodded. "Technically, around here we've just got the county sheriff's department and the state police. I'm not sure how that works, but Terre Haute has the closest larger city police force, so you might be able to pull from their staff."

"Can you tell me about the people who will be around this place on a daily basis? This is a bigger operation than I expected when you said 'family farm.'"

Coulter smiled, and Ross read the genuine warmth and affection in his expression. He really loved this place. "This is my wife's family home. You've already seen the bed-and-breakfast and Storybook. There's also a petting zoo, a huge plot of organic crops—mostly sold at farmer's markets and in a subscription service. Poppy's parents, Laura and Keith, still live on-site."

He ran through the list of people quickly, and Ross struggled to keep up. Coulter gestured at the notebook. "I'm sure Andi can provide all this information."

Coulter was probably right, but Ross liked collecting his own intelligence as much as possible. "I'll confirm my list with that one when I get it. Go ahead."

"My brother-in-law Hawthorne is the operations

manager. He'll have any information that Andi doesn't have. There are at least a dozen other employees that I don't really know. Part-time college students who help with animals and crops."

"And your house is on the property somewhere?"

Coulter nodded. "We're on the back acreage. It's away from the main part of the farm, but still connected. Depending on the day, we might be at our house, at the main house with Laura and Keith, or visiting the animals. Poppy says it's important to give our kids the full experience of growing up on the farm, even if we spend a big portion of our time in the city."

Ross nodded. That was a really wholesome goal. He hadn't met the governor's wife yet, but from everything he heard, she was smart and kind. "Just so you know, our protection doesn't technically extend to your children. Just your wife." He saw Coulter's smile falter. "When your children are with you or your wife, they will have the protection of the detail. But while they are alone or with other family members, we don't have personnel attached directly to them."

"Okay, that makes sense. Thanks for letting me know. I never considered what that looked like."

"Obviously, we hope it never becomes an issue,

but if there were a breach of security or an immediate threat—our team will do whatever it takes to protect you and your wife—and your children. But our first priority will always be you."

The governor nodded, but Ross could tell this conversation had put a damper on their meeting. He looked around the barn. "Maybe we should take a break. I need to grab a bite before my meeting with the head of security this afternoon."

Coulter nodded. "Sounds good. Why don't you come back to our house for lunch? There isn't anything to grab as far as takeout within about a fifteen-minute drive. I'll text Poppy really quick and let her know."

Ross started to protest, but the governor was already standing up and pulling out his phone. This was fine. He needed to see their house anyway, and to meet the first lady.

He wrote a few more notes and shut his notebook. "Should I go grab my car? I left it at the bed-and-breakfast."

Coulter waved a hand. "Nah, you can ride with me and I'll just tell Andi to pick you up at our house instead." Harrison tucked his phone back into his pocket. "I'm going to go grab Maggie and we'll head out."

Ross strolled around the barn, admiring the large chandeliers and the huge wooden beams that spanned the vaulted ceiling. He noted the open loft over one side of the barn. That would be important to secure during events, and a good location to observe from. An elevated vantage point would give his team a helpful perspective, in addition to eyes on the ground.

Lily walked out with Harrison and Magnolia.

"Bye, Maggie. Thanks for all your help! Come see me again."

"Are you sure you don't want to come for lunch?" Harrison asked her.

"I'm actually headed into town to meet Josh for lunch."

"Ah, I see how it is. I'll just tell your sister that you'd rather hang out with Josh than her."

Lily chuckled. "I'll call her later. It's probably time for a girls' night."

"I want to come to girls' night!" the young girl shouted.

Coulter winced. "Maggie, watch the volume."

"Sorry, daddy." Immediately she turned back to her aunt. "Can I, Aunt Lily? Can I come to girls' night? I'm a girl!"

Ross smiled at her enthusiasm.

"You are a girl! Of course you can come. Maia will want to come, too, I'm sure."

"Yay! Did you hear that, Daddy? Maia and I can come with Aunt Lily and Mommy and Daisy and everybody!" Maggie was still chattering her excitement as they drove from the barn to the Coulter home.

Ross looked out the window, adding more questions to his list for Andy.

7

*A*ndi was sitting with her mom in the dining room when her phone buzzed with another text message. It seemed like the whole farm was in a tizzy about Agent McClain, who'd shown up late last night. She heard all about Agent McDreamy from Daisy in a string of text messages that didn't die down until nearly 10:00 p.m. Then this morning, she'd already heard from Lily and from Harrison.

She had been gearing up for her meeting with the head of Harrison's protective detail for a week or two, buttoning up every gap in security she could identify and rectify on such short notice. Things weren't where she would like, but it had come a long way since she arrived.

This Agent McClain better not be another

egotistical musclehead with more brawn than brains. Not that the Secret Service typically hired morons, but some people were better at hiding their inadequacies. Still, she was trying to be positive. It was going to be fine.

She had just as much authority on this property as they did.

Kind of.

"You seem distracted, sweetie." Her mom's gentle probe brought Andi out of her musing.

"I'm fine. Big meeting later with the Secret Service guy."

"Oh, Daisy told me about him. She said he was very nice and a little intense."

Andi raised an eyebrow. "Is that all she said?"

Her mom blushed. "Well, he is apparently very handsome as well."

Oh, great. Daisy's big mouth had put ideas of matchmaking in her mom's mind.

"Mom..." she warned. "Don't even start." Her mom had already made a few hinting comments about how Andi should get to know their new produce manager, TJ. Andi had met him, but the guy was ten years younger than her and there was nothing there to pursue.

Not that Andi needed to pursue anything. She'd

been mostly alone for her entire life. Coming back to Bloom's Farm wasn't some plea for help in her dating life.

"I'm just saying, maybe you'll have more in common with this man than the men around here."

"He'll only be here for a few months, and he'll probably be on the road with Harrison for most of it anyway."

Her mom held up her hands in surrender. "Okay, okay. I just want you to be happy."

"I know, Mom. I am happy though. There are a lot of things that keep me up at night, but the direction I chose for my life is not one of them." Bad memories came with the territory. God had been faithful in granting her peace though. She knew too many of her Army buddies who still struggled with the mental impact of surviving in a war zone.

"We're so proud of you, Dandelion. I hope you know that."

Andi nodded. "Thanks, Mom. I'm glad to be home." While they finished their lunch, Harrison sent a text that she should pick up the lead agent at their house on the back part of the property. Andi stopped by her current bedroom in the basement to grab her notebook. Then she grabbed the keys for her father's side-by-side from the hook by the garage door. She'd been using it as her own since coming home.

Andi pulled up in front of Poppy and Harrison's farmhouse. It looked like it belonged in a magazine from the outside, and Andi knew the inside was a comfortable mix of modern farmhouse and the typical clutter that came with a house of kids.

The front door opened, and Harrison stepped out, looking every bit the politician and lawyer he was, despite his jeans. A man in khakis and a button-up shirt followed close behind. He finished saying something to Poppy behind him and turned to face her.

Andi felt her stomach drop and her mouth fall open. "Ross?" She lowered her voice and spoke to herself. "You've got to be kidding me, God." Had he planned this?

Angrily, she pulled the key out of the ignition and stomped around the vehicle toward the porch. She ignored Harrison's confusion and Poppy's undisguised interest in the scene playing out before her.

"Andi?" He sounded surprised, but she didn't let it slow her down.

She grabbed Ross's sleeve and pulled him back inside the house, forcibly directing him into the small office space that sat to the left of the entry.

She whirled toward him. "What do you think you're doing here?"

He raised an eyebrow. "My job." He crossed his arms.

Andi forced her eyes away from the way his biceps strained against the short-sleeve dress shirt.

"This is my home. You shouldn't be here." Everything about this felt wrong. Her life in Virginia was a thousand miles away. It always had been. And now this man, who had gotten under her skin so thoroughly while sparring—was here?

"Look, Andi, I don't like this any more than you do. But I serve my country however they ask me to, and for now that means I'm in charge of protecting the governor and his wife."

She took a deep breath and tried to quiet the clamoring objections going on in her head. He was serving his country. She understood that, right?

Maybe she did, but Andi couldn't shake the feeling that Ross McClain was an invading force, a hostile takeover of her home base. It didn't help that Harrison and Poppy had been laughing with him like McClain was their new best friend. Daisy had already gushed about the guy. And all of this without Andi realizing that Agent McClain was one and the same as Kohai Ross from the dojo.

She huffed. "Fine. You can stay. But only because you're protecting Harrison and Poppy. And I kind of like them."

Her eyes moved to his lips as they twitched. Bad idea.

"Such hospitality." He continued in a dry, sarcastic voice, "It's making me feel all warm and fuzzy."

Andi stepped close and looked him in the eye. He had her by a few inches, which irked her, but she held strong. "It will never be my goal to make you feel all warm and fuzzy. Got it?"

"Yes, ma'am."

She narrowed her eyes, unable to tell if he was being sincere or sarcastic. Probably better not knowing. Andi stepped back and sighed. "I guess we better do what you came here for."

He gestured to the porch through the window where Poppy was not-so-casually standing and looking through the window. "You going to explain to them, or should I?"

"There's nothing to explain. We know each other —barely–from Virginia. That's all."

"Suit yourself, Andrea."

For the love of Pete. "My name is Andi. Or better yet, Sergeant Major Bloom. Got it, Ross?"

He crossed his arms again. "Since we're being professional, you can call me Agent McClain. Or you can call me boss. Since I'll be in charge of the security on-site for the next several months and I'll need you to follow orders, soldier."

Andi called on every ounce of self-control she'd mastered through her years of training. She stepped back instead of lunging toward him. The truth was, she didn't use violence as an answer. And even though she knew McClain could handle it, knowing that he was likely to dodge or block her hit made the idea of striking out far less appealing.

"I'm retired. And you're not my commanding officer." She leaned against the armchair in one corner of the room. "How about this? We both have the same goal—to keep Harrison and Poppy safe, right?" When he nodded, she waved a hand. "As long as we are both on the same page as far as the mission, let's not get hung up on who is in charge."

Especially since she wasn't about to take orders from a glorified bodyguard.

ANDI DIDN'T WANT to get hung up on who was in charge? He could play along. Especially since he had the authority granted by the Department of Homeland Security, and Andi had... a tiny office and a radio he could buy at the nearest electronics store.

"Works for me." He stepped across the room to close the distance between them. "I have to say, it was really fun to be your opponent at the dojo. Perhaps it will be just as fun to be on the same side this time."

Her mouth opened and closed several times. Ross felt a surge of satisfaction at making this woman —who always seemed to have an answer for everything—speechless. He turned on his heel and headed out of the room, leaving her behind to contemplate his comment. Actually, he didn't know why he said that. If anything, Andi Bloom was going to make his job a hundred times more difficult. He didn't know anything about her, other than she was an excellent and accomplished fighter, and apparently held the esteemed rank of Sergeant Major.

So perhaps she wasn't the most inexperienced security personnel he'd ever worked with, but sometimes that was worse. At least when people knew they didn't know anything, they stepped aside and let him work.

He had a feeling Andi would rather be forcibly

removed than step aside and let someone else take command. Frustrating, infuriating, stubborn woman.

He stepped back onto the porch for the second time. Mr. and Mrs. Coulter gave him questioning looks, and he shrugged. "Old friends."

Andi scoffed behind him. "You wish." She shoved past him and climbed in the driver's seat of the UTV. "Get in, McClain. We're going shopping."

What on earth was she talking about? There was laughter from his left, and he looked at Mrs. Coulter for help. "Did I miss something?"

"It's from a movie. Don't ask."

Alrighty then. He jogged down the steps and climbed in. When Andi pressed the gas and the vehicle jerked to a start, he grabbed the handle above the door. Was she trying to kill him? They jostled down the gravel drive while Ross said a prayer for safety. He considered asking her to slow down, but that was exactly what she wanted, wasn't it? This was a test. It was a tactic to see who would cave first and show weakness.

Well, it wouldn't be him. He tightened his grip on the handle.

"So, when did you leave Alexandria?"

Andi glanced over at him like she'd forgotten he

was there. "What? Oh. I moved home at the end of June."

That was right after they exchanged the paint. "Oh. I didn't realize you were moving. This seems like a nice place."

She narrowed her eyes. "Don't try to small talk me. I'll tell you about Bloom's Farm. You'll bring in all your stuffy robots in suits to stand around and look intimidating and we'll both make sure nothing happens to my sister and her husband."

Ross pushed down the irritation. It was a simple comment, for crying out loud. "Fine. Tell me what I need to know." He was going to have to listen carefully, because writing notes on this carnival ride of a drive wasn't going to happen.

"I've only been here a month, but I've already made quite a few changes I think you'll agree were necessary. We've upgraded all the home security systems. That covers the bed-and-breakfast, the main house where my parents live, and Poppy and Harrison's house."

Ross nodded. He'd noticed the control panel near the front door.

"Eventually, I'd like to get the other houses hooked up as well, but they weren't a priority."

"Other houses?"

"We each have about five acres of our own." She pointed to the right where another gravel drive split off. "They are hard to see through the trees at Poppy's house, but the houses all branch off this road. Hawthorne and Avery's house is back here. We already passed Lavender, Daisy, and Lily's places. Rose sold hers back to the farm when she moved to Montana.

Ross's head was spinning. "Geez. So many flowers. What's up with that?"

"Long story."

He listed off what he remembered. "So... Governor Coulter is married to your sister—Poppy. Then there is Daisy, Lily, and Lavender." He put up a finger with each name he said. "Who am I missing?"

"Rose and Hawthorne."

He paused a beat. "And you."

"And me," she confirmed.

"So your name isn't Andrea."

"I told you it wasn't."

"It's got to be a flower, right?"

"Drop it, McClain." Her voice held a heavy dose of warning in it.

He tried to think of all the flowers he knew, but couldn't come up with any that would be shortened to Andi. He knew that the routine background check on any of the Bloom siblings would also reveal her full name, but he couldn't help but want her to trust him enough to share it. They would have to do a check on her as well, but he had a feeling she wasn't going to like it.

"I don't understand why it's such a big deal to you, but I am going to have to run a background check on everyone at Bloom's Farm. And that includes you."

He saw her adjust her grip on the steering wheel. "When?"

He wasn't sure what he'd been expecting, but it wasn't that. "Um, probably in the next week."

"Okay."

"So you're not going to tell me?"

"I'll take that one extra week where I get to keep my secret."

"If you'll recall, technically you already lost a bet and were supposed to tell me then."

She groaned. "I forgot about that."

"So what's it going to be, Andi. Are you a woman who sticks to her word?"

"I really don't like you."

He laughed. "I can't say I'm your biggest fan

either. But I will find out your name one way or another, so you might as well tell me."

She mumbled something under her breath.

"Sorry, what was that?"

"I said it's not a flower." She looked at him, but he wasn't sure how to respond. "My name. It's not a flower. It's a weed."

"Huh?"

She sighed. "Daisy, Lily, Lavender, Poppy, and Rose. All beautiful, feminine floral names. And over the years I've come up with at least a dozen others my parents could have chosen for me. But instead, they chose a dumb weed."

"So your name is...."

She let the vehicle roll to a stop. Then she squared her shoulders and turned toward him with her hand extended. "Dandelion Bloom, reporting for duty, sir."

It took every ounce of self-control for Ross to school his features and not betray his initial reaction to her name. "Nice to meet you, Dandelion."

She rolled her eyes. "Now you know. And now you may never call me by that name again. I go by Andi. Always."

He nodded curtly. "Okay."

She started driving again, and they sat in silence.

A few moments later, he spoke again. "It's not as bad as—"

"Can it, McClain."

Her tone left no room for argument. She would have been an intimidating commanding officer. "Yes, ma'am."

8

*R*oss listened carefully as Andi showed him around the rest of Bloom's Farm from the side-by-side vehicle. At least she had slowed down. As she talked through the upgrades she had already made to the security system, he had to admit he was impressed. The woman knew her stuff.

"Tell me about your background. Sergeant Major Bloom... Army?"

"Transportation Corps," she confirmed. "Before Belvoir I was at Fort Bragg with the 82nd Airborne. Before that I was based in Germany, deployed to Afghanistan with Combat Support. Twenty years of service, three tours, and a lot of pushups."

Ross mentally adjusted his expectations of Andi Bloom. Her experience wasn't marginal at all. In fact, he could argue that her security expertise, being based on hostile territory gave a perspective he could appreciate, but not imitate. There were different challenges when things appeared safe—agents letting down their guard was one of the most common. The people he protected were, by nature, constantly put into vulnerable positions and constantly convinced nothing would go wrong.

"Three tours? Wow. Thank you for serving. It couldn't have been easy."

Andi shrugged. "You serve too. Nothing any of us do is easy. But it is necessary."

There it was—a slight shift in the energy between them. A begrudging respect instead of a stubborn distrust.

"I think the biggest challenge for security here will be large events not related to the governor. I don't suppose Lily would let us cancel all the weddings on the calendar from now until the election?"

Andi's laughter caught him off guard. Had he heard her laugh before this? It was a melodic, light sound that made him want to make it happen as often as possible. It seemed Andi didn't hand out smiles or affection readily. He shouldn't be thinking about how much he wished that smile could be directed at him.

"Not a chance on God's green earth. Some of those weddings have been on the books since the spring before last. Lily would tear you apart for even suggesting it."

He sighed. "I figured."

"But that's not your biggest security concern, anyway."

He whipped his head up from the notebook where he was writing a note about wedding security. "It's not?"

"Nope. Think about it. Weddings have guest lists. Easy enough to get from the bride and verify ahead of time. And that's only a concern if Harrison and Poppy are on-site." She pulled up in front of an open field. On the opposite side stood rows of trees.

"Welcome to the orchard—the site of Apple Picking Days, the pumpkin patch, and the occasional bonfire."

"So?"

"So this is your biggest security concern. I asked Lavender; last year Apple Picking Days saw three thousand visitors over seven days. No tickets are sold ahead of time, and we have no way to tell who will be here and no way to stop any potential threat from showing up. And it is in four weeks."

"So we'll just make sure the governor is somewhere else that week."

She grabbed her phone and pulled something up before handing it to him.

He groaned when he saw Governor Coulter's social media post, made yesterday. The campaign was supposed to clear all events through their team, but more often than not in these cases, the plans were already made before he got a say. It wasn't the end of the world—he probably wouldn't have vetoed the Apple Picking Days event. It would be similar to many of the rallies on the campaign trail—no guest list, a wide-open field, and a lot of people.

"I guess we're working Apple Picking Days."

"Let me know what you want from me."

He glanced at Andi. The truth was, he didn't know what he wanted from her. He had a feeling it was a lot more than she was willing to give though.

"Is there a dojo around here?"

Andi shook her head. "There are a couple of karate studios in Terre Haute, but nothing at your level. Closest thing is an MMA gym. I haven't gone yet—I've had some bad experiences, and grappling isn't my thing. I've been considering starting one."

He understood. Rolling around on the floor with sweaty guys wasn't exactly his favorite thing either. And unless you were fighting someone with a lot of experience, a takedown and a simple armbar were enough to incapacitate them. She sounded sad about the lack of options for true martial arts practice. "If you want to go work out at the MMA gym sometime, I'd be happy to go too. Maybe we could have a rematch."

The corner of her mouth lifted for a beat, then resumed her typical resting scowl. "Probably not. Thanks for the offer though."

He shrugged, though the rejection stung. "Offer stands. I'll be here for a while, and I wouldn't mind a chance to practice as well. Katas in my hotel room get old quickly."

Ross wasn't sure why he was so determined to win Andi over. She clearly didn't like him. And when he looked at it from a distance, he couldn't say he really liked her either. She was closed off and gruff. She rarely smiled and thought she knew best in every situation. But there was something about her hard shell that only made him want to see what was inside, behind her tough exterior.

What was going on behind that noncommittal expression of hers? Did she have any of the same tumultuous feelings about him? Or was it just like it seemed—that he was nothing more than an inconvenience in her role as head of security?

AFTER SEVERAL HOURS of riding and walking the farm with Agent McClain, Andi dropped him off at the bed-and-breakfast. Daisy bounced down the steps with an exuberant wave. "Agent McClain, I see you met my twin sister, Andi."

McClain laughed. "Sure did. You could have given me a heads up when I called you Andi last night."

Andi's eyebrows flew to her hairline. It wasn't a huge surprise that he would mistake Daisy for Andi, except that despite being identical twins, they looked quite different these days. Daisy's face and figure had rounded out with the arrival of Brielle. Plus Daisy kept her hair long and mostly wore it down. When McClain had sparred with Andi in Virginia, her hair had been even shorter than it was now.

Daisy, however, was clearly unapologetic. "It was way more fun this way. How do you two know each other anyway?"

Andi jumped in before McClain could say

anything that would give Daisy extra ammunition for teasing her. "We don't. We met a couple times back in the city, that's all."

Daisy raised an eyebrow at McClain, who shrugged. "That's true." Then he leaned in and stage-whispered, "We were dancing partners."

Daisy's eyes were saucers when she turned to Andi with a gasp. "Dance? You went to a dance class and didn't tell me?" Her voice jumped three octaves as she asked the question.

Andi groaned and glared at Ross. "Now look what you did. Daisy, no. He means we sparred. Like hand-to-hand combat. Definitely not dancing."

Daisy's body slumped in disappointment. "Aw, man. Well, it's still cool that you know each other. It's always nice to have old friends visit the farm." Daisy winked at Agent McClain, and Andi tried to set her sister on fire with a look.

"That's enough, Daze. We met once. Not friends."

McClain shrugged. "That's true. She doesn't even like me." It was Daisy's turn to give a disapproving look.

Andi smacked a hand on her forehead. What on earth was McClain thinking? He was giving Daisy the entirely wrong idea. "You two are the worst. I'm leaving. McClain, I'll see you tomorrow."

"Thanks for the tour, Andi."

Andi didn't respond as she threw the vehicle into gear and spun the tires as she drove away. McClain better get his act together. This wasn't some game for her—it was her life. And he might get to leave in a few months when the campaign was over, but she would have to live and work here. And giving Daisy the wrong idea about the two of them would only cause trouble.

She didn't understand him. Sometimes, he was so rigid and professional and sometimes he cracked a joke that had everyone in the room eating out of the palm of his hand. She could relate to the Agent. She just couldn't relate to the man.

Which was a problem, because she found herself wanting to see a whole lot more of both of them.

9

McClain liked his role as team lead. It meant he wasn't always the one standing up on stage next to Governor Harrison, but he was in on the logistics and strategy of the entire protection detail.

It was a lot to manage though. He looked at the next month of events. Ten days in Indianapolis, ten days at Bloom's Farm, and two five-day road trips—one through the Rust Belt, and one through Texas and the South. His team was gathered in the small trailer he'd had delivered to Bloom's Farm and parked behind the bed-and-breakfast.

Claussen, Ridgeway, and Stapleton sat at the table across from him. Ten additional team members were on video chat. They were the advance team, already on-site at half of the upcoming locations. Rogers was on duty guarding the residence and would be briefed later.

He'd been on enough assignments to understand how to structure his team. Unless there was a campaign event at Bloom's Farm, there would only be two agents here. Same with Indianapolis. There wasn't enough of a consistent threat here at the farm to warrant additional agents, and the state police had the capital covered well.

The travel locations were the biggest priority. He would be with the governor at every stop, and his team would leapfrog ahead of them on the road.

As long as Coulter or his campaign manager didn't get any crazy ideas about adding events last minute, they would be okay. The team ran through the schedule for the next five days, walking through all the protocols and contingencies for Coulter's protection. Today, the governor was hosting the Governor of Texas, hoping to convince the oil industry giant to endorse the campaign.

"Everybody good?"

Nods from around the room.

"Good. See you tomorrow—same time, same place."

The morning briefing was a routine he appreciated. In his work, Ross was nothing if not regimented and methodical.

Like he had the last three days, he prepped for his morning meeting with Andi. As head of security for the farm, they needed to be in constant communication. Honestly, sometimes he felt like his entire job was just talking to different people so everyone was on the same page.

He checked his watch when Andi poked her head in the trailer door. 7:57. Andi seemed to live by the Army saying "If you're not fifteen minutes early, you're late." Usually, she was pacing outside of the trailer, waiting for him to wrap up with his team.

"I thought maybe you forgot about me."

She raised an eyebrow. "I wish. Just a little behind this morning," she said.

He tried not to let the barb sting. They'd found a comfortable place working together over the last few days, but there hadn't been much to discuss. Today was the first day something was happening on the farm that really required a protection detail.

He rolled his shoulders back. More than he needed her to like him, he needed her to listen. There was nothing he took more seriously than his job. He knew even though it shouldn't, he even let his faith take a backseat to his role as a Secret Service Agent.

"Let's get started then, shall we?"

ANDI PUSHED DOWN HER IRRITATION. As much as she wanted to pretend it was Ross's comment that had her riled up, the truth was that she hated being late and couldn't stop kicking herself for getting distracted this morning. Her impromptu morning time with her father had been precious, but it had also put her behind schedule.

She was itching to get back out to her office and finish installing the monitoring software that would go on every computer the farm owned.

Checking her watch, she tried to focus on what Ross was saying. The man could rehash the same information fifteen times. Meeting every morning, it seemed like they had the same conversation every day. She knew he was just making sure everyone was on the same page, but she was more of an action-oriented person.

"I'm going to need you to escort Governor Parsons and his team to Governor Coulter's residence. They are expected to arrive at nine this morning."

Andi's eyes flew to his. "Why do I have to do it?"

"It makes sense for someone from the farm to greet them, instead of an agent. Coulter will be at the house waiting, with Ridgeway and Claussen on duty."

"And Rogers? Can't he escort the team?"

Ross's jaw tightened, and he set down his pen and folded his hands. It reminded her of the school principal she'd managed to cross a time or two. The epitome of control.

"Sergeant Major, I'm relaying the assignment you've been given as an extended member of Governor Coulter's security team. Are you capable of fulfilling that assignment?"

Oh, now he'd done it. He knew darn well she was capable of more than being the resident tour guide. And invoking her rank? Agent Ross McClain was on her territory. This was her farm and her family. And as much as he might think so, she had no intention of blindly following orders from him.

She debated briefly trying Lavender's sugary sweet tactic, but instead went back to her usual forceful demeanor. Ross wouldn't buy a syrupy smile from Andi anyway. "Agent McClain, if you believe I am simply another underling you can order around and move around on your tactical map, you are sadly mistaken."

Perhaps it was cliché, but she pointed her finger and pressed it into the table to punctuate her point. "This is my farm. And I do not appreciate being treated like some low-level security guard. If you have something you'd like me involved in, you are welcome to include me in the discussion from the beginning. If there is a change of plans, I am happy to step in and stand in the gap wherever it is needed. But you will not send me here and there as you please."

Ross bristled and leaned toward her. "I don't know exactly what you think is happening here, Andi, but I'm simply trying to do my job. I couldn't care less if you feel slighted because I didn't ask your permission to give you an assignment. It's not my job to protect your feelings—just the lives of your sister and brother-in-law. If you have a problem with the way I'm doing my job, you're welcome to remove yourself from your position. Because I can promise you, I'm not going anywhere until this election is over and you have zero authority to make me. Got it?"

Andi fumed. The nerve on this guy.

The worst part? He was right. She had no authority. At least not while he was here. And as attractive as the idea of him leaving was, she didn't doubt him when he said he was here to the end.

She crossed her arms. Then she uncrossed them —afraid she would look like a petulant teenager. "Next time, I'd appreciate more than an hour's notice if you can help it. I have things to do as well."

Ross nodded. "That's fair. And I will bring you into the planning phase earlier any time I can."

"Thanks."

He held her gaze and Andi stared back, unwilling to blink. This version of Ross? The brash, no-nonsense commander... She knew how to handle those types. She'd been doing it her entire career. It was the funny, disarming, friendly guy that some-times showed up outside of business hours that she struggled with. That guy made her feel all tangled up inside, and she didn't know how to handle that. The Ross sitting across from her right now just made her want to spend extra time kicking the snot of out a heavy bag.

"Okay, where were we?"

It wasn't that Ross didn't understand where Andi was coming from. He did. He just also couldn't worry about that when he was coordinating his staff and schedules.

Andi was just going to have to suck it up and deal with the fact that he was in charge. He'd do his best to loop her in when he could.

"I'm escorting the Governor of Texas to the house."

"Right. Then Ridgeway and Claussen can take it from there. Apparently they've got horseback rides and some skeet shooting."

Andi chuckled. "I wonder if Harrison will pull out the cowboy hat."

"Does he have one?"

Andi shrugged. "Probably. His dad owns cattle. Even though Harrison became a bigshot lawyer, he's got country roots."

"I noticed that." Ross met her eyes. "He seems like a decent guy."

"For a politician, you mean?"

There was no humor in Andi's response, and Ross shook his head. "No. I mean as a person. He seems like a good one."

Andi nodded. "I had my doubts once upon a time, but yeah, I think you're right."

Ross's curiosity was piqued. "Doubts?"

"It's a long story. But it had a happy ending. Harrison is solid."

There was more to it, but he got the very distinct feeling Andi wasn't going to let him behind the curtain. Which didn't matter. Because this was just work.

Ross's phone rang. He glanced at it, then looked at her. "It's Coulter. Just give me a sec." Then he answered the phone. "McClain."

He froze when the governor's words registered. "We've received a threat."

en minutes later, McClain pulled up to the Coulter house with Agent Ridgeway riding shotgun. She was a good agent and would provide a sympathetic presence for Mrs. Coulter as they walked through this threat.

He spared a glance toward Andi's UTV, parked next to the front steps. How had she beaten him here? Also, how did she even know to come? As much as it had killed him to play it cool and dismiss her without the info, until he had a handle on it, he couldn't bring anyone in. Not without clearance. No doubt she would be ticked, but he didn't have time for egos this morning.

He briefly wondered if there was any way he could get her clearance increased for the assignment.

There was a stipulation about private security consultants. He'd look into it later. For now, she'd just have to wait in line.

When Mrs. Coulter opened the door, she led them back to the living room, where Governor Coulter and Andi were waiting. Someone was on the speakerphone of Coulter's cell, and Ross quickly recognized the voice of Coulter's campaign advisor.

"This happens all the time, Harrison. Don't let it worry you. Remember how—"

Coulter glanced up at him and cut off Neil Powers. "Thanks, Neil. Agent McClain is here now. I'm going to bring him up to speed. I'll call you back later." Without waiting for a response, Coulter ended the connection. Ross had to admire the man's command. He was clearly used to holding power. Whether or not he used that power responsibly still remained to be seen for McClain. But, with the job, the politics didn't matter. He'd protected foreign leaders that he knew were absolute dictators. It wasn't easy, but it was the commitment he'd made.

"Governor, you remember Agent Ridgeway? She will be on your traveling detail, along with myself and Agent Claussen."

Coulter stood to shake her hand. "Thank you for what you are doing for me and my wife."

"Okay, tell me what happened."

"The threat came to our Facebook. We get a lot of angry messages, but this one was different. Here, take a look."

Poppy showed him the laptop. He winced at the photoshopped image of Coulter. "Is that...?"

"It's a butcher shop."

"Okay, then. Definitely different from your usual dissenter comments. I'll send this back to the investigative team in Indianapolis to see if they can determine where it came from."

"So you think it's a real threat?" He could hear the apprehension in the petite woman's voice.

Agent Ridgeway spoke calmly. "The odds of someone acting on a threat like this are close to zero. But we take every threat seriously and we will do everything in our power to apprehend the person responsible and to protect you both."

Mrs. Coulter nodded and Ross noticed the governor lay a comforting hand on her knee. "It's going to be okay, sweetheart." She laid her hand on top of his and squeezed.

He swallowed thickly. He saw a lot of political couples in his role, and it was rare for one to display the connection he saw between Mr. and Mrs. Coulter.

Andi cleared her throat and he turned. She'd been silent until now, but she spoke to the governor and her sister. "Harrison's right, Poppy. It's going to be okay. We won't let anything happen to you." Then she leaned toward them. "Do you want us to pray together?"

Despite all his training, Ross knew his face would betray his surprise at the offer. His impression of Andi took on another layer. She was a believer too.

Mrs. Coulter nodded gratefully and the family all ducked their heads. McClain did the same. He had never prayed with a family he was protecting before. There were plenty of times he had prayed for them and for his team though.

Andi's prayer was short and precise, but obviously sincere. She spoke with the confidence of someone who came to the Lord often. He couldn't help but admire her courage to immediately offer prayer in a tough situation like this. Would she have done the same if it hadn't been her sister?

When the prayer ended, Mrs. Coulter wiped her eyes and stood up to hug Andi. "Thanks, Andi. I'm glad you're here." Then she turned to him. "I'm glad you're here, too. We're trusting that God put each of you in this place for a reason."

He nodded, then his gaze shifted to Andi before he could stop it. "I think so too."

ANDI PACED the small office where her security system was housed. She'd torn down the wall between the two offices and Hawthorne had helped turn them into one larger space. The ancient desktop computer monitor had been replaced with a panel of flat screens, a revolving series of live images from around the property.

The threat against Harrison and Poppy had shaken her a bit. It hit differently when it was her family. There'd been plenty of dangerous situations while she was deployed, but that was to be expected. She'd been mentally prepared for that. This, on the other hand? Perhaps she should have expected it. Political views were a touchy subject and plenty of citizens felt strongly enough about the issues to resort to violence on their behalf. But she hadn't expected it.

Just like she hadn't expected McClain. She was increasingly both frustrated with him and his controlling ways and intrigued by his character. He'd bowed his head and prayed with them this morning.

Did that mean he was a believer? Or just that he thought it would be rude not to?

A knock on the door interrupted her pacing, and she turned to see the very object of her thoughts staring back at her.

"Have a minute?"

"Sure you want to invite me to this conversation?" She raised an eyebrow. When she'd gotten the call from Poppy, she'd rushed to their house. It wasn't until later that she realized McClain had received the same call and not told her what it was about. She'd been in the same room with him, for crying out loud.

"That's not fair, Andi."

"Oh, come on, McClain. Just admit you messed up."

He shook his head. "It wasn't my place to bring you into that conversation yet. I'm glad your sister called you, but if she hadn't—there is nothing I could do about it. I would have briefed you later."

"Would you? Or would it be need-to-know?" He pressed his lips together and she continued, "That's what I thought."

"It's not personal, Andi."

"It sure as heck seems that way. This is my farm. My family. If there is something going on, I expect to be informed." She was inches away from him now. Her finger pressed into the fabric of his shirt near his heart.

Gently, he grabbed her hand and removed it from his sternum. "I understand. I already decided that we need to get you listed for clearance. At Governor Coulter's request, there shouldn't be any issue with it."

She exhaled and spoke curtly. "Good. Thank you." She moved to take a step back and felt the tug on her hand. He still held her hand in his. Andi shifted her gaze from their hands to his eyes.

They were kind and gentle as he whispered, "I'm sorry."

Nothing could take the wind out of the sails of her outrage like an apology, and she felt the tension drain from her body. "It's okay. I understand. It's protocol."

He nodded. "It is. But it still sucks sometimes."

She let a burst of laughter escape. "Yeah, it does."

He released her hand, and she immediately missed the warm, gentle touch. That awareness made her step back. She needed space between them, fast. "Did you stop by just to apologize?"

He shook his head. "Not entirely. You still good to escort Governor Parsons at nine?"

She bristled at the unneeded reminder. "I said I would. And I will."

Ross held his hands up in surrender. "Just making sure. I also wanted to let you know I was leaving. The governor is going back to Indianapolis tomorrow after he finishes up with Governor Parsons, and I'll be going with him."

"What about Poppy?"

"Mrs. Coulter is staying here. Agent Rogers will be with her."

"So Ridgeway will be with you?"

"She is," McClain responded. He definitely didn't seem disappointed with that assignment. Andi fought down the jealousy that threatened to rear its head. The female agent was young and attractive. Despite the suit, she was soft and smiled easily. It wouldn't be hard to understand if McClain had feelings for her.

"She seems like a good agent," Andi choked out.

There was a hint of amusement on his face when he replied. "She is."

He had better not be laughing at her. Andi turned back to her screens. "Well, have a good trip."

Andi watched his reflection in one of the monitors, but refused to turn back. It seemed like a long time before he finally left. When he did, she sagged into the chair. What was that all about? Her body was betraying her, reacting like a hormonal teenager, for crying out loud. And jealous? McClain would never jeopardize the mission by getting involved with Ridgeway. Of course, that also meant he would never jeopardize the mission by getting involved with her. Which wasn't disappointing to her. At all.

He would be gone for a few days. Maybe that would be enough to get him out of her head. She took a deep breath and tipped her head back to stare at the ceiling.

It seemed increasingly unlikely that it would be that simple.

Ross WALKED BACK from Andi's office at Storybook Barn toward the bed-and-breakfast. The Governor of Texas would arrive in thirty minutes and he couldn't spend anymore time thinking about Andi. At least not until later. Heaven knew he'd get lost in the middle of his katas tonight and find himself picturing Andi instead. At least, that's what had happened the last two evenings.

Ridgeway and Claussen were at the Coulter residence. They would need another agent to accompany the governors on their horseback ride while Ridgeway stayed with the wives.

Claussen hadn't been thrilled with the assignment. Apparently, he had a thing about horses. McClain had just laughed, but told him he could ride ahead on a four-wheeler.

Then he'd told Ridgeway to keep an eye out. There was something going on with Claussen, and if he couldn't figure out what it was soon, he was going to have to pull Claussen off the team. It might just be a distraction at home, but a distracted agent was a threat all its own.

On the walk, he pulled out his phone and called Gallo.

"Did you see my email?"

"I got it. You've got Indianapolis working on it?"

"Yeah, I do. Can you do me a favor and see if we have anything else in the system that matches this MO though?"

"Sure. You think it's credible?"

"Honestly, I'm not sure. It seems just odd and specific enough to have legs though. You know?"

"Your gut?"

"That too."

"I've learned to trust that gut over the years. I'll do some digging. Everything else okay?"

"Just fine. Governor Parsons is here today, and then tomorrow we head to Indy for a night before we hit the road and head up to Michigan."

"Team in place?"

"Of course." McClain tried not to let the simple questions bother him. Gallo was just covering the bases, but if McClain didn't have a team in place already, he would be falling down on the job.

"Sorry, I know you've got this, but I've got to ask."

"Feel free to jump on our morning calls any time you want to check in on us."

"Is that a six a.m. call?"

McClain smirked. "Sure is."

"Hmph. Don't hold your breath."

He laughed. Gallo wasn't exactly known for being an early riser. "Wasn't going to."

"Just keep me posted. Any update on the leak?"

"Nothing. I've got my suspicions, but I've got nothing substantial to back it up."

"Didn't I just say I've learned to trust that gut? Tell me what you're thinking."

"I'd rather not. No point in casting suspicion on someone that might be innocent."

"Okay, but don't lose focus. If there is something off, we need to address it."

"Understood."

When they disconnected, McClain stepped inside the bed-and-breakfast and spotted Daisy.

"Agent McClain, how is your afternoon?"

"Do you ever leave, Mrs. Matthews?"

She smiled. "Sometimes. But I love it here, so I try to be here as much as possible."

"Can you do me a favor?" She nodded and he continued, "I need your reservations for the next four weeks. I need to run background checks on anyone staying here at the same time as the governor or his wife are on the property."

Daisy bit her lip. "Am I allowed to give you that information?"

He smiled. "Yes. If you'd rather, I can give you a list of specific dates and you can just provide the information for the days in question. I just thought it would be easier if you just provided the data all at once."

"It's fine. I just didn't know. I'm a business owner, after all. I don't know what I'm allowed to share legally."

"Unless something is classified by the federal government as Top Secret, I'm pretty much allowed access to anything required for my protection mission."

"I guess that makes sense." Daisy shrugged. "Send me the dates, and I'll provide you the names of all my guests."

"I'll need names and addresses."

"Sir, yes sir." Daisy saluted him with gusto.

"No salutes here. That's your sister's domain, not mine."

"Oh yeah? What does the Secret Service do, then?"

He tapped the side of his nose like he was signaling their conversation was a secret.

"Ohh." She mimicked the motion with a wink. "Got it."

"Speaking of Andi..."

It was probably a mistake to bring it up, but Daisy was suddenly very interested. "What about her?"

Ross scratched his head. "I don't know. Does she hate me?"

Daisy smirked. "Let me tell you a story about my husband, Lance. Have you met him yet? No? Well, you need to. He's the best guy in the world, but there was a time when we met that I would have sworn up and down that I hated the guy. Truth was, I couldn't handle the fact that I wanted to hate him, but couldn't." She held up her hands. "Now, I'm not saying that Andi does or doesn't dislike you. I'm just saying that sometimes, feelings are harder to differentiate than we realize."

Well, that made perfect sense. He did not like Andi. Or at least he didn't want to like her. The problem was, the woman was becoming far too likeable with every moment they spent together.

11

*A*ndi watched with minimal interest as a car entered Bloom's Farm and followed the drive toward the petting zoo. Perhaps she had overestimated the need for security at Bloom's Farm. Or at least her ability to be the one monitoring it.

Since she started, she had enjoyed the process of improving the systems, training the employees, and working large events. The day-to-day stuff though? It was kind of mind-numbing.

She stood and stretched. With a quick hello to Lily, she walked outside and did a few laps around Storybook Barn. She glanced at the side-by-side, but decided a drive wouldn't do it either. Instead she slowed her breathing and stepped into the rhythmic flow of her katas. Maybe she could get a martial arts bag and set it up somewhere on-site. They were kind of bulky, but striking the dummy was a lot more satisfying than hitting the air like she was doing now. And neither was quite as satisfying as striking Agent McClain.

She leaned back and pressed her heel up and forward in a kick. Then she brought her foot down and punched the air with her left hand, feeling the stretch in her shoulders.

A few minutes later, she disappeared into the movements, her mind erasing everything else beyond the familiar patterns of kicks, steps, punches, and blocks.

"Bend your knees, Bloom."

The voice jerked her out of the zone and she wobbled as she kicked, staggering to catch herself before she fell on her butt.

"What the—? McClain, don't sneak up on someone like that." Her face was burning with embarrassment. Her heart raced, but she wasn't sure if it was the scare or if it was the realization that he was back on the farm. He and most of the team had been gone for four days. A very long four days. They'd exchanged several emails about security on the farm, but Andi was hesitant to acknowledge that she kind of missed her orders being delivered with

McClain's signature no-nonsense tone. They made her want to reply with a snarky comment once the meeting ended.

He held up his hands. "I wasn't exactly sneaking. I drove up and even slammed my car door. You must have really been centered."

Andi narrowed her eyes. It didn't *sound* like he was laughing at her. In fact, it almost sounded like he admired her. "I was," she said cautiously.

"I've never been able to get out of my head enough to do that."

"Do you meditate?" The question slipped out before she had a chance to think about whether it was a wise move.

He shook his head. "You mean like sit cross-legged and say ohm?"

Andi smiled briefly. "That's one meaning. But that's not exactly what I do."

Ross stepped closer, his voice quiet. "Would you teach me?"

Andi silently inhaled a surprised breath. Was that... humility? "Umm, I guess I could. It's sort of a Christian thing. I mean, it might work with some-thing else, but that's how I learned." She fidgeted nervously and lowered her eyes. She wasn't ashamed of her faith, but she didn't want to make other people uncomfortable either.

Ross ducked into her view. "That sounds great. I'm a believer too." He smiled. "Actually, I wanted to tell you I appreciate how you prayed for the governor and Mrs. Coulter last week."

Andi shook her head. "It was no big deal."

"It was a very big deal. It takes a lot of courage to pray in front of people you don't know. And it takes a special faith to turn to prayer first, instead of as a last resort."

Ross reached for her hand and she jerked it away. Immediately, she felt a surge of regret. It had been a reflex. And though he was trying to play it cool, Andi saw the flash of hurt in his eyes when she'd pulled her hand away from his.

"McClain, I'm—"

"It's fine, Andi. I'm a big boy." He turned back toward his car before calling out, "I will take you up on those meditation lessons though." Then he lifted a hand in a wave without turning back to her.

"I'm sorry," Andi said quietly to herself. He didn't stick around to hear the apology, but it didn't make it less true. She didn't apologize often. But the truth was, if she could do it over again, she wouldn't pull her hand away from Ross. And that was a real-ization she wasn't sure what to do with.

Ross SLAMMED the door to his sedan and trudged up the steps to the bed-and-breakfast. When he'd spotted Andi working out in front of the barn, he'd been helpless to resist stopping to see her. Four days on the road with the governor was nothing compared to what he was used to, but he found himself hoping Coulter would spend more and more time at Bloom's Farm. It was easier to protect him here. At least that's what Ross was telling himself.

Andi was just a pleasant distraction. Or unpleas-ant. Definitely that. Right?

Daisy called a greeting, but he waved and kept walking directly up the stairs. He couldn't help it. He was kind of irked by Andi's rejection at the barn. She'd pulled away from him like he was a leper and this was old testament Jerusalem.

Was he really so repulsive to her?

He pulled off his shoes and let them fall to the floor. He shouldn't care so much about her reaction to him. But for once in his life, Ross wanted someone to look beyond his suit and like him. At work, he needed his team to trust him and respect him and listen to him. But like him? That didn't really matter.

For some reason, he wanted Andi to look at him without getting the feeling he was gum on the bottom of her boot.

His phone rang and Ross answered it with a fatigued greeting. "This is McClain."

"Whoa. You all right?"

Gallo's voice made him sit up straighter. "Yeah, I'm fine. Just got out of the car. What's up?"

"I've got some info on that butcher hook threat."

"Just a second." Ross pulled his notebook out of his bag, then picked up the phone again. "Okay, what do you have for me?"

"The IP address used to send the message came from public Wi-Fi located at a coffee shop in Chicago."

"Hmm." That wasn't great news. Chicago was a big city and not very far from here. It didn't narrow down their suspect pool at all, and it meant the governor was within easy driving distance whenever he was in Indianapolis or at Bloom's Farm. He pulled out the schedule.

"We've got an event in Chicago in two weeks."

"I know. That's why I wanted you to know.

You'll want to make sure the Chicago office has extra personnel for that event."

"Got it. Anything else you know?"

"Not yet. We're working on getting video from the coffee shop for the time the message was sent, but they aren't exactly fans of the government. The warrant is just taking a little time."

"Okay. Let me know when you have something else. Can I loop in the team?"

"All clear for your team and the team at the capitol."

"What about Andi? I mean, Miss Bloom—the head of security here?"

Gallo paused. Ross knew he had tripped up, calling her by her first name. Had his boss picked up on that as well?

"Yeah, that's fine. Looks like the governor added her as his personal security consultant and requested she have full access."

When the call ended, Ross's mind flooded with all the implications of knowing the threat came from Chicago. He pulled out his laptop and quickly scheduled calls tomorrow with the team in Chicago and the team in Indianapolis. Then he called Andi.

"This is Andi."

"This is Ross. Umm, Agent McClain."

"Hey 'Ross, umm, Agent McClain.' Didn't I just see you?" Her joking tone made him smile, and he wanted to respond with friendly banter of his own, but it wasn't the time.

"Yeah, actually I've got some news on the threat against Harrison. Can we talk?"

Her tone was immediately all business. "Of course. Do you want me to meet you at the trailer?"

Ross was grateful for the temporary base of operations, but he dreaded the closed-in, beige interior of the trailer. "I'm at the bed-and-breakfast. Why don't we just chat in the sunroom?"

"I'll be right there."

Seven minutes later, Ross settled into a cushioned wicker armchair in the sunroom, which was decorated in vibrant blues and greens and filled with plants that gave the room a cozy summer atmosphere.

Andi stepped in, talking to someone inside as she did. "I'm not going to do your dirty work, Daze. If you're going to miss brunch, you'll have to tell Mom yourself!"

Andi let the door close behind her, the trace of a laughing smile still on her lips as she turned around. It disappeared quickly though. Ross grounded himself in the business of the hour by gripping his notebook tighter.

"Thanks for coming."

Andi shrugged. "Of course. Tell me what's up."

Ross walked through what he had learned, emphasized that the information was classified except to those on the Secret Service team. "That means you can't even tell your sisters or brother."

His eyes fell to her lips as they tugged to the side in the hint of a frown. But she nodded in acknowledgement. Another thing he liked about Andi. She might not like it, but she would follow orders. Just like him.

"Okay. I will double check that we don't have any guests for upcoming weddings who are from Chicago."

"That's a good start. I would also like you to track all the license plates of visitor cars to the farm. Most offenders will visit prior to an attack for planning."

Andi nodded and wrote herself a note. When her eyes flipped up to his, he saw the fear in them. "How serious is this, Ross?" His name on her lips revealed how impacted she was by the situation, and he'd be lying if he said the sound of it didn't affect him.

He leaned forward, their knees almost touching.

"It's probably an empty threat. But we will take it seriously in case it turns out to be something real."

Andi pressed her lips together. "She's my sister. This is my home."

"I know it's scary. But you've been through worse."

"Not here."

Despite the voice of proper protocol screaming within him not to do it, he laid his hand on hers. "I trust you without reservation. But if you need to step aside, we can find someone from the agency to step in for Bloom's Farm."

Andi shook her head adamantly and took a shaky breath. "No. This is my responsibility. I feel like God specifically brought me back here for this, you know?"

He heard her words, but his eyes were on their joined hands. She hadn't pulled away.

"I understand. And I think you might be right. Your family is very lucky to have you."

She gave him a small smile, and he allowed himself to enjoy the little victory. "Thanks."

He took a deep breath and gathered his courage to say what was on his mind. "I know we've gotten off to a rocky start. And I think I'm right when I say that I'm not exactly your favorite person." She snorted a laugh and he grinned. "Okay, maybe that's an understatement. What I'm trying to say is that we might not see eye-to-eye on everything, but I think we make a good team."

Andi's eyes were on their hands. "I'm not usually a very good team player," she said quietly.

He squeezed her hands. "Neither am I, to be honest. Unless it's part of following orders, I'd much rather take everything on solo."

Andi met his gaze, and he saw a vulnerability in them he had never seen before. "Gets lonely, doesn't it?"

His heart stuttered. "Yeah," he admitted. "It does."

Andi lifted one shoulder and tilted her head down to it. "Maybe... maybe it doesn't have to be? If you can find the right teammate."

He desperately wanted to tell her she was right. That maybe with the right teammate, it wouldn't be so lonely, and that it could work. But even with the feel of her hand in his, and the way her eyes were locked on his, the only thing he could think to say was the one thing that would ruin their chance.

"We can't," he choked out.

The hope in Andi's eyes dimmed, and he kicked himself for his lack of tact. "What I mean is... you make me crazy, in the best way. And we do make a good team. Professionally."

"Oh." She pulled her hand from his and straightened in her chair.

Oh, he was screwing this all up. "Trying to be something more would just be a distraction, you know?"

"Sure. I get it."

"I'm not sure you do." He grabbed her hand again. "I'd very much like to continue to get to know you better. But until this campaign is over and I am no longer protecting your brother-in-law... We can't do anything more."

There was a flash of understanding in her expression now. "So maybe after...?"

"Absolutely. After." Without a doubt, he hoped she would still be interested after. A lot could happen between now and then.

"Okay."

"Until then... we'll just be colleagues and maybe get to a point where we don't make each other want to scream in frustration?"

Andi flashed a wide smile that took his breath away. She was strong and smart. And stunning.

"I'd like that, Agent McClain."

He missed the way his first name sounded on her

lips, but it was probably better to keep it professional. "Sergeant Major Bloom," he replied with a wink. He loved the way her cheeks tinged with pink at his flirting. "For now, let's focus on protecting the governor. Then we can focus on the rest."

12

When Andi saw the dark gray smoke rising behind the tree line, she wasn't concerned. It wasn't unusual to have a burn pile stacked out in one of the pastures from downed limbs and cleared underbrush. But Hawthorne hadn't mentioned anything about burning this week. And it had been kind of dry. It seemed like odd timing. Hawthorne might not always be the most cautious individual, but he wasn't careless.

Andi grabbed the radio from her belt. "This is Andi for Hawthorne."

There was a beat of silence before his response. "Go for Hawthorne."

"Hey, are we burning something on the southwest corner?"

"What? No, there are no scheduled burns. You got eyes on it?"

"Headed that way. But it's sure making a lot of smoke whatever it is."

"I'll call it in and meet you out there."

Andi turned the side-by-side off the gravel drive onto a rutted dirt path that led around the border of the property. The smoke wasn't coming from the houses on the back acreage, nor were they from either of the barns. In fact, she couldn't figure out what was out that far, other than crops. Was there a wildfire in one of the groves of trees that lined the fields?

As she got closer, she realized where the smoke was leading her.

She crested the hill and her heart sank. Smoke trailed skyward from the long rows of trellises as fire consumed the vines and posts of Poppy's personal vineyard.

She turned left and saw the fire was inching closer to the small wooden barn where Poppy housed the winemaking supplies. She hadn't used it in years, instead selling the grapes to others. But she would be devastated to lose this little piece of the farm that had always been her special place.

Andi called on the radio again. "Andi for Hawthorne."

"What's out there, Andi?"

"It's the vineyard. Getting close to Poppy's barn."

"Fire department is on their way. I already got a text from Bryce Storm. He says he's on the truck and they've got the tanker."

"Tell him to take County Road 1100 instead of the main entrance to the farm. It'll get them here faster. I'll go open that gate. If they get here soon, they might save the barn."

Andi covered her mouth with her shirt as she drove around the vineyard toward the road. She opened the gate, grateful she had replaced all the locks with matching padlocks. Hawthorne pulled onto the shoulder of the county road in his truck and she walked out to meet him, hanging her arms on his open window frame.

"How bad is it?"

She glanced back toward the field. The flames were licking up the side of the barn, but mostly the damage seemed on the field. "I don't know. I hope Bryce gets here soon though."

The siren of the fire truck reached her first, then finally, two large red vehicles turned the corner. She stepped out and directed them through the gate. Hawthorne followed on foot.

The firefighters sprang into action, but Captain Storm came over to them. "Anybody inside?"

She shook her head. "Shouldn't be. It's locked up. Poppy has the only key."

"Okay, good. My guys will do a 360 and we'll give you an update. The field might be a goner. What's beyond that tree line?"

"Orchard."

"We'll do our best to keep it isolated here. You've got a dry hydrant, right?" She looked at Hawthorne and prayed he knew the answer.

"It's between the main house and the barn. I can show you."

"Our second tender is on the way. If we empty this one, we'll need to fill it at the hydrant while we drain the second. It's been so dry lately, we don't want anything else to catch. What was growing here, anyway?"

"Grapes."

"Huh. Alright. Stay back and let us do what we can."

Andi stood by, feeling helpless as she watched the Minden-Rogers Fire Department hauling hoses, soaking the ground and spraying down flare-ups.

Storm came jogging back. "The barn is in good shape. That south side caught on the exterior, but no evidence that it penetrated the building. We'll hose it down on that side, then we'll need to go in to make sure it didn't catch inside."

"Oh, thank goodness." Andi exhaled a sigh of relief.

The thick gray smoke began to thin and be replaced with steam. It quickly dissipated as the grapes burned themselves out and the firefighters quelled the burning grasses near the edge of the field.

She knew they'd had the occasional fire on the farm over the years. A field of hay that was baled a little too wet and got too hot could catch on fire easier than a book of matches. One year, some kids had set off fireworks on the back corner of the property and managed to burn down a grove of trees before it burned itself out. But this was the first time Andi remembered a building being at risk.

A flash of movement got her attention, and she saw Storm waving her over. She nudged Hawthorne and headed that way.

"Did you see the back of the barn when you pulled in?"

Andi frowned. "No. Did it burn after all?" Bummer. Poppy was going to be really disappointed.

Captain Storm shook his head. "No. It's fine." He tipped his head. "Come on back and take a look."

Andi followed him to the far side of the barn. The dripping red paint was stark and eerie against the faded gray of the old barn, and her heart sank.

Stepping back, she took in the message someone had left behind.

Their blood is on your hands.

Without hesitation, Andi turned to her brother. "Hawthorne, I need you to call Poppy and tell her about the field. Don't mention the message."

She turned back to Storm. "Thanks for everything. We need your team to keep this part of the fire quiet. Don't mention this to anyone. I've got to call the Secret Service and let them know what happened. Can you stick around to talk to him?"

"Sure, Andi. No problem. I'm really sorry we couldn't save the vineyard."

"You guys were awesome. Now that we know the fire was set on purpose, we've got bigger problems than those grapes."

After making sure Captain Storm could stay, she pulled out her phone and tapped on Ross's contact info.

"Agent McClain."

"Where are you?"

"I'm at the trailer doing some scheduling."

"There's been a fire. I need you to meet me at the vineyard."

"There's a vineyard? Did we see that?"

"It's such a small, unimportant part of the farm, I never even thought to show it to you on the tour. It's important to Poppy though. And the culprit left a message."

"What kind of message?" His tone was clipped and business-like.

"Can you just come out here? I'll meet you at the produce barn and drive you back here."

"I'll head that way."

She hung up and waved for Bryce's attention. "I've got to go pick up Agent McClain. I'll be back in 5 minutes."

"I'll be here. I'm sending the rest of my guys back to the station though. Shift ends in 2 hours and they'll have a lot of work to do getting the truck restocked."

"No worries. Tell them we appreciate it—and if anyone asks, it was just a normal burn that got out of control."

He gave her a thumbs up and Andi climbed into her UTV and drove to pick up Ross. He was waiting for her beside his car, parked in front of the large barn used for the produce operation.

She pulled in next to him and he climbed into the passenger seat without a word.

On the way back to the vineyard, she brought him up to speed. "I saw the smoke about an hour ago. I called Hawthorne, thinking we might just be burning a brush pile or something, but usually he lets everyone know if that's the case."

She slowed down to lessen the jostle from a particularly bad bump in the rutted path. "Anyway, he said there was nothing scheduled, so I went out to investigate. Poppy's vineyard was on fire and it was getting close to the little barn she used for equipment. We called the fire department in and they got things under control."

"You said there was a message?"

She parked the vehicle safely away from the still smoldering vineyard. "Yeah. I didn't see it until Captain Storm pointed it out."

She led him around to the far side of the barn and watched his features as he surveyed the scene. His jaw tightened and he swore under his breath. "Why didn't you call me sooner?"

Her mouth fell open. "What?"

"The person is long gone by now! You should have called me as soon as you saw the smoke."

Andi reared back in surprise. "This is not my fault, Agent. And I'll have you know that I called you as soon as I realized this wasn't just some normal farm occurrence. Things catch on fire, McClain. Want me to call you next time a cow dies? Or next time a tractor breaks down?" She stepped closer, unwilling to back down. "I had no reason to think this was related to Harrison. And as soon as I knew, I ignored my desire to call Poppy myself and I called you instead."

Ross just shook his head and pulled out his phone to take photos of the vandalism.

Andi marched away. Big, dumb, bossy jerk. She'd done the right thing. There hadn't been a reason to call him.

She was muttering to herself when Bryce came up next to her.

"He seems pretty intense," he commented.

Andi scoffed. "Yeah, you could say that."

"Of course, everybody around here is watching Harrison's career. Governor was one thing, but this whole vice president thing is pretty crazy. Someone from our neck of the woods might be in the White

House? But I guess I didn't think about all the bad stuff that comes with it."

She nodded. "It's a big deal, for sure. Agent McClain might be intense, but he knows what he is doing." Even if he's a big jerk while he is doing it. "It's still a little crazy to think my little sister has a Secret Service detail."

Storm chuckled. "I could see that being a bit surreal."

As they chatted, Ross came up. "You're the firefighter that found the message?"

"One of my firefighters, sir. I'm Captain Storm. Nice to meet you. Andi was just telling me how good you are at your job."

Ross raised his eyebrow at her. "Was she? Well, that's reassuring. Did you happen to see anything else that made you think the fire was started intentionally?"

Captain Storm shook his head. "I'm not really sure. Vineyards aren't exactly conducive to widespread fires. Unlike fires in alfalfa fields and such, where the plants are so close together—the vines should burn and spread slowly, since they have to follow such a narrow path along the trellises." He looked back at the field. "It looks like the grass was a little long, but nothing that I would have been concerned about. So yeah, it doesn't seem like an accident. Based on the burn patterns, it looks like someone set the vineyard on fire from multiple points around the exterior."

Andi listened with interest. Bryce sounded like he knew what he was talking about. McClain was taking rapid notes.

"Can you walk around and show me where you think the fire was lit?"

"Sure." The three of them circled the barn, and Storm pointed out the positions where they'd identified additional burn patterns. "See how this trellis post is burned out significantly more than the others down the line, or even the ones on either side?" He held the back of his hand to it, then flipped his fingers over, touched the burnt wood, and then brought his fingers to his nose. "Smells like lighter fluid."

This was worse and worse. "So someone soaked the trellis in lighter fluid to start the fire?"

"Not just this one. Look," he pointed down the edge of the vineyard, along the first post of each row. "Every 4th or 5th row was torched. Then, the fire spread along the grass to the other rows, and migrated down the rows toward the opposite end of the field. The only reason the barn was even in danger was because the fire spread through the long grass between here and there."

"You see much arson around here?"

His eyes widened, and he shook his head. "No, sir. Sometimes kids might light up an old shed in someone's pasture, but usually it's because they are playing with fireworks in the wrong spot." He tilted his head and looked up. "Bill Prater burned down his own barn a few years back, hoping for an insurance payout."

Ross wrote down the name and Andi rolled her eyes. "You can't possibly think Bill Prater did this. The man's sharp as a marble, but he's not dumb enough to threaten a vice presidential candidate."

McClain gave her a look. "I'm just being thorough, Sergeant Major." His tone gave no room for argument and Andi clenched her teeth to keep from making a smart aleck remark. He turned to Bryce. "Thanks for the info, Captain. This was really helpful. Do you happen to have any special arson training?"

Storm stood up straighter at the praise. "As a matter of fact, I took a course in Indianapolis from the IMFD Fire Inspector last year."

"That's great. Thanks for sticking around to show me what you found too. We're going to need you and your crew to keep quiet about this. Not the fire, since I'm sure that's already got the rumor mill working overtime. But about the message on the barn. It's a matter of national security, you hear?"

"Oh, yes sir. Absolutely."

Andi nearly gagged. Could Storm be any more of a suck up? McClain was clearly pandering to the eager firefighter.

"You need anything else from the Captain, Agent McClain?"

Ross narrowed his eyes at her emphasis on his title. "Nope, all set here. If I have any more questions, I'm sure someone around here knows how to get in touch."

She turned to the firefighter. "Thanks for everything, Bryce. Say hi to your brother for me."

"You got it, Andi." He smiled. "It's good to have you back. You know, I was starting to think I'd never get my shot with any of the Bloom sisters."

Andi's mouth nearly fell open, but she schooled her features. How should she respond to that? Bryce was a nice guy. A few years younger than her, and he had certainly grown up since she remembered him at church youth group. "Umm..."

"Don't worry about it. I know you've got a lot on your plate right now. But think about it, will you? If

I'm not at the firehouse, I work at Brand New Land-scaping."

She heard a cough from Ross behind her. "Good to know," she said noncommittally. Then she had an idea. "You know, maybe I should get your number. You know, just in case we have questions about the case. Or whatever."

Captain Storm smiled broadly and rattled it off as she put it in her phone. Then he walked back to the red fire department pickup truck.

She slid her phone back into her pocket and turned back to Ross.

He stood with his arms crossed. "What was that all about?"

"What was what all about?"

"You getting his number."

She shrugged, trying not to laugh. "I figured it would be good to be able to get in touch with him. He did seem to know a lot about the fire."

Ross harrumphed, like a grumpy old man. Was that jealousy?

"Do you have a comment, Agent McClain?"

Ross took a deep breath. Did he have a comment? It had surprised him how much he'd been bothered when Captain America had flirted with Andi.

He tucked his notebook into his pocket. Andi was staring at him with her hands on her hips, a challenge in her eyes. He loved the way she never backed down.

But he wasn't one to back down either. He glanced around. They were alone.

"No comment," he said, as he took a step closer.

She raised her eyebrow. "Are you sure? Seems like you have something to say."

Another slow step. He shook his head. "Nope. Nothing to say."

Andi tipped her head back to maintain eye contact as he drew closer, the space between them all but disappearing.

"I really don't like you sometimes," she said.

"I really don't like you sometimes either," he replied, just before he lowered his lips to hers and cut off her reply.

Their kiss was a battle as much as it was an alliance. After a small gasp of surprise, she kissed him back, as though actively searching for something just out of reach. Her hands came to his shirt, and he thought she might push him away. Instead, her fingers twisted into the fabric, holding him firmly in place.

It was as though their lips waged war, each trying to gain the upper hand. All the frustration and tension and stubborn arguments came to a head. Just when he thought she had surrendered entirely, she pressed forward again. Softly, he tucked his hand under her ear and around her neck and gentled his kiss. He wrapped his other hand around her waist. No pressure, just a caress. He surrendered to the tumult of emotions that came with her nearness. And in response, so did she. The fervor of the kiss faded into a whisper. She hummed, almost a whimper of need. He tasted her lips gently, and rubbed her cheek with the pad of his thumb before pulling back to meet her eyes.

They fluttered open—unfocused, soft pools of cool, green glass.

"On the other hand... sometimes, I really like you," he said with a hint of a smile.

"Umm." Andi blinked and started to pull away.

He held her in place. "Wait." He kissed her again. "Don't run away, Andi. This doesn't have to be scary."

But when she tried to create distance between

them this time, he didn't resist. Immediately, he missed the warmth of her body against his. She turned away from him, and he waited for her to say something. The last thing he wanted was for her to shut him out. After a kiss like that, he didn't see how she could.

Her hair fluttered in the cool breeze as he waited. Finally, she spoke, her words quiet as she faced the vineyard. "What was that, Ross?"

Ah, there it was again. His name.

He smiled and joked, "I'd be more than happy to show you again, Andi." Anytime, anywhere.

She whirled around, her face far more distraught than he would have expected. "I'm not joking! This isn't funny to me. Is this a game to you? I thought we couldn't. I thought I was a distraction?"

"Whoa. I'm sorry, Andi. I was just... I didn't mean to act like it was no big deal. And you *are* a distraction. But I can't seem to mind that right now. I can't seem to think of anything beyond how badly I want to make you smile at me again. How badly I want to kiss you again." He took a cautious step towards her. "Don't you feel it too?"

She shuddered with a heavy breath. "That's not the point. We've got to protect Harrison and Poppy." She gestured wildly at the vandalized barn. "Look what happened! Someone came on to my property and destroyed something that Poppy loves. I failed."

He pulled her into his arms. "You didn't fail, Andi. And we will find who did this and protect your family. I promise."

She tucked her head under his chin and he pressed a kiss to her hair. "You're probably right. This wasn't the time or place. But my feelings for you don't take away from my ability or desire to do my job. In fact, they only make me more determined to protect the people you care so deeply about. It's not only my honor on the line if something were to happen. It's also your heart. And I would never want to let anything hurt you."

As he spoke, Ross realized just how true his words were. This assignment was personal. It wouldn't cloud his judgment, but it was sure going to make him work harder than ever to make sure he didn't miss anything.

He pulled back and lowered his head to meet her eyes. "Are we a team?"

She nodded. "Absolutely. Let's catch this guy."

13

*A*ndi paced the table in the small meeting room of the trailer. Photos of the vandalism and the fire spread across the table, along with maps, lists of past arsons in the state, and any information on the threats against Harrison.

It looked like every cliché scene from a crime procedural she'd ever watched. All that was missing was an unnecessarily large headshot of Harrison taped to the white board. She picked up a map of Bloom's Farm and studied it. Poppy's house. The vineyard. All the locations where Lindsey had game cameras were marked, but there was nothing close to either location.

"Let's go over what we know," she suggested.

Ross rubbed his temples with his fingers. "We've got the Facebook message. What did it say again?"

Ross had promoted Ridgeway to take the lead on events and travel that extended beyond Bloom's Farm. His entire focus was the threat against Harrison, and for that, Andi was eternally grateful. Agent Claussen was here too. The more help, the better.

Claussen found the printout and read the message. "Your success comes at their expense. You'll pay for this. Then the photoshopped image."

"Okay. We've got two possibilities. Either the message and the fire are linked. Or they're not."

Andi had been thinking the same thing. "I don't know. Both of the messages seem so random. I don't see how they are linked. Neither of them makes much sense, actually. Harrison has a super high approval rating. He doesn't have any nefarious business background where he's exploiting people or anything. In fact, he came into the spotlight for standing up to corrupt organizations. He's the hero of the story, not the villain."

Ross shook his head. "That depends on who is writing the story. Obviously, someone sees him as the villain. We just have to figure out who it might be."

Claussen jumped in. "So you think it's one person?"

"That's what my gut says."

Andi frowned and crossed her arms. "Well, my gut says they aren't linked. And I'm way more worried about someone who came onto our property and is willing to set a fire!"

He stood up and walked toward her. "You are right. The arsonist is definitely the bigger threat." Did he say she was right? Andi felt her heartbeat slow. Then he continued, "We will focus our efforts on that. But if they are the same person, the other threat gives us context that could help us find the culprit."

She took a deep breath. "Fine. But I think we're wasting our time looking at this photoshopper."

"It's never a waste of time to run down every lead. Tunnel vision never helped an investigation."

Ugh. That was true, but Andi wasn't sure she wanted to admit that.

Ross turned to Claussen. "Can you go check in with the computer forensics team and see where they are with the image and the Facebook message?"

"On it." Claussen disappeared into one of the offices the agents shared and shut the door.

"You're right," she admitted begrudgingly once they were alone.

He smiled at her. "Was that so painful?"

"Excruciating," she confirmed, with a hint of a smile. "Let's do it your way."

"You're pretty cute when you're compromising."

Her mouth fell open in surprise. He kissed her quickly, stifling any argument.

"Just take the compliment, Bloom."

"Sir, yes sir," she said before kissing him again.

Ross hung up the phone. The Chicago office had gotten him a list of known and suspected arsonists residing in the Chicago area. But it was a very long list. Too long to be helpful at this point.

He was still missing something. What was it? His gut was telling him there had to be a connection between the Facebook threat and the message left on the barn.

Your success comes at their expense. Your blood is on their hands. The photo of the butcher shop. Did it mean anything? Or was it just a graphic way to say they wanted to hurt Harrison?

A knock sounded as the door of the trailer opened. Andi stepped inside with her laptop tucked under her arm.

He gave her a tight smile. "Got anything new?"

She grinned at him. "As a matter of fact, I do. The vineyard is on the very back corner of our property. It used to be trees, but Poppy had that portion cleared. The neighbors still have a big swath of woods back there. I thought it was a long shot, but I remembered Buck was a big hunter, so I thought maybe... Turns out, I was right. He's got a trail camera set up in the woods across the fence from the vineyard, so I asked if it picked anything up on the day of the fire. Check this out."

She opened her laptop and showed him a picture. The photo was blurry, but the image was clearly a woman. She wore a baseball hat, baggy pants, and a long sleeve shirt.

"She cut through the woods?"

Andi nodded proudly. "I figure she didn't want to park on the county road by the farm, so she pulled off onto Buck's access road and parked there, then hoofed it to the vineyard."

"Nice work."

"Thanks. I thought maybe we could narrow down our arsonist lists to female perpetrators and go from there?"

He nodded but continued to stare at the picture. "That's a good start. Most arsonists are repeat offenders." He tapped the screen. "You see her shirt? Can you read it?"

The shirt had some sort of logo or words on it, but it was cursive and hard to read.

Andi leaned in and clicked to zoom in. She squinted at the screen. "Meat is... something. Murder?" She gasped. "Meat is murder!"

Ross felt a flood of adrenaline as the clues fell into place. The photoshopped butcher hooks, the message about blood. Except, what was the connection to Coulter?

"So...This person is threatening the governor because... Bloom's Farm raises livestock?" He let his doubt color his tone. That hardly made sense. From what he'd seen, Bloom's Farm's livestock operation was extremely limited. It was sustainable and free-range and there was far more focus on the petting zoo. Surely the animal rights folks had bigger concerns than this place.

Andi frowned. "I guess so. That does seem crazy though. Poppy was always focused on the produce anyway."

"I mean, this lady did start a fire. So crazy is in the profile."

Despite his words, there was still something nagging him. A vague memory of something he'd read. "Coulter's bio. Quick! Tell me everything you know about Harrison Coulter. Start at the beginning."

Andi counted facts off on her fingers. "He grew up around here. Rich kid. Became a lawyer and settled in Terre Haute. His grandpa was the governor a million years ago. His dad still runs the family ranch."

There it was. "Ranch?"

Andi's eyes widened. "Of course. Coulter Ranch is one of the biggest cattle operations in the state. They're huge. And they sell *a lot* of beef."

Ross slapped a hand on the table. "That's it! Whoever this person is, she's got an issue with the way the Coulter family makes their money. It doesn't matter that the governor has nothing to do with his family's business. I've got to get this information over to the team at the FBI. Using all of this information, we should be able to get a lock on her identity." He kissed Andi hard on the mouth. "You're a genius. Dinner later?"

Without waiting for a response, he jogged out of the trailer and headed to his room to make the calls he needed to. Finally, they had a lead on the woman behind the threats. Now hopefully, they could better predict what she would do next.

THROUGH THE WINDOW, Andi watched Ross go through the back door of the bed-and-breakfast with a blank look on her face. That had happened quickly.

She glanced around the now-empty trailer, and the papers spread across the conference table. On the wall, the calendar of events caught her eye. She quickly read through the list of upcoming events. Where would this woman strike next?

She ran her finger down the list, hoping something would stand out, but there was nothing remarkable about the list of fundraisers and rallies filling Harrison's calendar for the next month.

Andi sighed in frustration. They had gained so much information, but they were still flying blind. She grabbed her laptop and drove the UTV across the property, stopping at Poppy and Harrison's house.

"Aunt Andi!" Magnolia's cheerful greeting lifted Andi's spirits.

"Hey, squirt. Is your mom around?"

"She's inside doing laundry. She said I can fold the dishtowels after she does the rest." Magnolia's voice held the pride and excitement only a five-year-old's can hold about something as mundane as laundry.

"Whoa. You know how to fold dish towels?" Andi infused the proper amount of awe into her voice.

She went inside the house and found Poppy exactly where Maggie had said she'd be.

Poppy looked up in surprise. "Andi!" Her excitement immediately turned to concern. "What happened? Is Harrison okay?"

Andi held up her hands. "Everything's fine. We've actually got some leads on the person threatening you guys. I wanted to see if you might have any ideas."

Poppy folded a small pair of jeans and set it on a stack of similar tiny items. "Let's go to the kitchen. You want a cup of coffee?"

"Nah. Honestly, I could really go for a Dr Pepper."

Poppy laughed. "Oh, my bad. I thought I was talking to Andi, not Daisy."

"Ha ha," Andi said dryly. "Water is fine." She sat at the bar and looked out the window at the kids. When Poppy set a Dr Pepper in front of her, Andi laughed. "You gave me a hard time and you actually had one the whole time?"

Poppy shrugged. "Daisy keeps them in my fridge for when she's here."

Andi chuckled. "Is there anywhere she doesn't keep it? She's probably even got a stash of Dr Pepper hidden out near the creek."

"Honestly, it wouldn't surprise me." Poppy sat across from her with a bottle of water. "So tell me what's up."

Andi laid out what they'd learned about the woman, based on the messages and the shirt. "Ross thinks she's some sort of animal rights activist targeting Harrison because of Coulter Ranch."

Poppy tipped her head, "Oh, it's Ross is it?" When Andi rolled her eyes, Poppy continued. "Okay, I'll let it go for now. But that's crazy. Harrison doesn't even have anything to do with Coulter Ranch."

Andi stole a line from Ross. "The woman set a fire. Crazy kind of comes with the territory. But can you think of anything that would help us find her? Anything about the ranch or about Harrison that I'm missing?"

Poppy tapped her fingers along the water bottle. "Oh my goodness. I was talking to Harrison's mom the other day. She was all worked up, telling me that their ranch website was acting funny. She thought it had been hacked. I, of course, assumed the network was down or something totally minor. I told her to worry about it when she got back from Colorado. If they did anything to the website, I bet no one has seen it yet."

Andi pulled out her phone. "It's definitely possible. No idea if this woman has the skills to do something like that. Let's see." She searched for Coulter Ranch's webpage and pulled it up, only to find a landing page plastered with the same photo of Harrison photoshopped on a butcher hook. Below it were big red letters. **Don't let blood money buy this election.**

"I've got to get this to Ross. If you think of anything else, let me know. And maybe tell his family to be careful. She's already set one fire."

14

_R_oss saw the text message flash from Andi. A website? He clicked through to the Coulter Ranch website and his eyes widened at the image and text.

The screen went dark and Andi's contact flashed. He accepted the call. "How'd you find this?"

"I told Poppy about the activist theory and she remembered Harrison's mom mentioning that their website had been acting funny earlier this week. When I went to look around, I found this."

A cyber-attack changed things. Anyone could send a Facebook message, but it took special skills to breach a website. "Hmm. I think we're looking at an organized group."

"What?"

"The profiles for an arsonist and a hacker are completely different. And if Arson Annie isn't working alone, then we have to assume we are looking at an organization of animal rights extremists."

He heard Andi swear under her breath.

"Hey, it's okay. This actually might be a good thing. If they are a bigger organization, it means they are on the FBI's radar. Which means we can share intel and act faster."

At least, that's how it was supposed to work. Somehow, interagency cooperation didn't always go according to plan.

"It just seems like more people who want to hurt Harrison would be a bad thing."

It had to be hard to be in her position. Being torn between wanting to do the best thing for the mission and having personal ties. It was one of the reasons he'd never wanted to get personally involved. "I know it seems that way. But more people mean more chances for a leak, intercepted communications, or an online presence. The most dangerous threats are solo attackers who operate in isolation."

"That makes sense. What do you need from me?"

Ross looked at his watch. Until they knew more,

Harrison and Poppy were well protected by the agents with him on the road in St. Louis, and the ones currently posted at her house. What he really wanted was to spend more time with Andi—without Agent Claussen in the way.

"Have dinner with me tonight?"

"You can't be serious."

"I'm totally serious. I'll get this info out ASAP, but then it'll be a waiting game while the FBI gets me what they have. Come on, have dinner with me?"

"Okay. I hope you like Thai food."

He couldn't remember seeing a Thai restaurant in Terre Haute, the closest large city suitable for a date. But that didn't mean there wasn't one there. "Love it."

"Pick me up at the main house at six?"

He grinned. "I'll see you then."

When Ross pulled up to the main house, he swallowed his nerves. It felt odd to be picking a woman up at her parents' house. But Andi wasn't just any woman. He'd met Keith and Laura Bloom once before, but it had been perfunctory handshakes. Since then, he'd mostly been isolated to the trailer or the bed-and-breakfast. Though he'd heard from Ridgeway that the Saturday morning brunch was something special. He'd told her she wasn't supposed to fraternize, but apparently the Bloom family was kind of pushy when it came to welcoming people. Would his welcome tonight be the same? Or was this like high school where her dad would be cleaning his shotgun at the table?

When Keith Bloom answered the door, all those images were immediately replaced by the joyful, vibrant guy in front of him. The white-haired man greeted Ross with a strong handshake and a one-armed hug before ushering him inside.

"Andi tells us you have been working night and day protecting Poppy and Harrison."

"Yes, sir. We have."

Keith's tone turned stoic. "Why aren't you working tonight?"

Ross's eyes widened. "Excuse me?"

Keith's serious expression cracked and he laughed. "I'm just kidding with you, Agent McClain. Even the man protecting my family deserves a night off now and again—especially if it is to take my dear Dandelion on a date."

"Da-ad."

Ross smiled at the way Andi sounded more like an exasperated teenager than a mature woman.

"It's your name, sweetie, and I'm going to use it."

"You can use it. He," she pointed at him, "cannot."

Ross smiled and held up his hands. "I wouldn't dare."

"At least someone listens to me," she said with an affectionate smile to her father.

"You two have fun," Andi's mother chimed in.

Ross followed her directions as she led him into a little town called Minden. He'd heard people mention it, but mostly he'd gone the other direction into Terre Haute instead. "There's a Thai restaurant here?"

Andi smiled. "Not exactly. My friend Chrissy owns a bistro here, and once a month there's a sweet Thai woman named Linda who takes over the kitchen and serves the best Thai food in western Indiana."

He parked on a quaint street decorated with patriotic banners, obviously still up from the summer.

Andi pointed down the block. "Minden Baptist Church is down there a block or two. It's where we went to church growing up."

"Do you go there now?"

"My parents do. The rest of us go to a bigger church in Terre Haute." She smiled. "We still come here at Christmas. I always thought I'd get married in that church."

That surprised him. Not necessarily because the dreams of a young girl were surprising, but because it seemed so unlike Andi to admit to having them.

His curiosity got the best of him. "Have you ever been married? Or close to it?"

Andi tucked her hand in his and they strolled down the wide sidewalk. "Not really. A few boyfriends here and there. But my career wasn't exactly conducive to long-term relationships unless the man was willing to follow me around."

"You could have married someone else in the Army, right?"

Andi wrinkled her nose. "Probably. Never found anyone that made me want to, though." She pointed at a sign ahead. "B&J Bistro is right up there."

Ross opened the door and let her walk in ahead of him. When they were seated, Andi asked, "What about you? Ever been married?"

"Seven times. But the next one is going to stick, I can feel it."

Her mouth fell open and Ross laughed. "Kidding, kidding. Never been married. Got close once, but..." he trailed off. What had happened to Candace still haunted him. Was he really ready to share that part of his past with Andi? She looked at him from across the table with a kind curiosity in her eyes. He took a deep breath. "She was murdered. We were engaged, but I was out of town on assignment and well... There had been a guy stalking her. The police were supposed to be keeping an eye on her, but they answered another call and the stalker came to her house."

"Oh, Ross. I'm so sorry."

"It was a long time ago," he said honestly. "Still, I'm not sure I really ever got over the fact that I protect people for a living and I couldn't protect her."

"It wasn't your fault."

"Sure it was. Sometimes, when I'm protecting politicians that are as crooked as a broken nose. Or even foreign leaders that are brutally cruel to their people... I think about how unfair it is that those people get a full security detail at the expense of the average taxpayer, and normal people are left to fend for themselves."

"So why don't you leave?"

He shrugged. "It's everything I ever worked for. Climbing the ranks of the Secret Service. Serving my country. There's got to be honor in that, right?"

Andi reached across the table. "Of course there

is. But there's honor in protecting the vulnerable too. We've both served our country for a long time. There's no shame in walking away to do something different."

Ross squeezed her hand. "Thanks." He let her words sink into his soul and comfort some of the ache there. He would always regret not being there for Candace. "I'll pray about it. I don't even know what it looks like at this point." The idea of leaving the Secret Service seemed completely foreign. And what would that mean for him and Andi? "You seem to have landed on your feet. Bloom's Farm and all that."

Andi shrugged. "Yeah, I don't know. I feel like without the whole campaign thing, there would barely be a job here. I've been thinking about opening a dojo. I could teach martial arts and self-defense. You know," she met his eyes, "help the vulnerable."

His heart warmed. Maybe they were more compatible than he thought. Was there something they could do together down the road? Between the two of them, there was a lot of expertise that had to be in demand. And they could help people too?

When the food came, Ross wanted to dive into the plate of basil stir fry because it smelled so good. They ate quickly, talking about their pasts.

"Siblings?" Andi asked him.

Ross smiled reflexively. "One sister, one brother. Rachael is the baby, almost ten years younger than me. Ryder is the quintessential middle child—a bit crazy and a lot of fun."

"Why am I not surprised that you are the oldest?"

He pretended to be shocked. "What is that supposed to mean?"

Her laughter made him feel like he'd won the lottery. "Oh nothing, Mr. Protocol."

"What about you? Tell me how all the Bloom siblings fit together."

"Lily's the oldest, then Hawthorne. Daisy and I came after that, followed by Poppy, Lavender, and Rose is the baby."

He frowned in concentration, trying to match the names with faces. "Have I met everyone?"

"Rose lives in Montana with her husband, Tate. Other than that, we are all pretty much centered around here."

"Wow. But you were gone for a long time, right?"

She nodded. "Yeah. Until Rose moved two years ago, I was the only one not living in the area. It was hard, but at the same time, I kind of liked that distance. Helped me avoid the drama."

"Drama? With your family?" he teased.

She laughed. "You have met Daisy, right? She's always in everyone's business. Trust me, I got the scoop most of the time."

"You guys seem very different." So different, in fact, that he'd immediately dismissed any relation, despite being twins.

"Ha, yeah. We are. But she's my best friend in the whole world. I know she'd move heaven and earth for me. Actually, any of them would."

"And you'd do the same." Ross had witnessed the love within the Bloom family. It wasn't something he saw every day. He and his siblings got along well, and he would do anything to protect either of them. But they didn't really know the details of his life, nor he theirs.

"Without question," she confirmed.

What would it be like to have that kind of devotion from someone as intense and dedicated as Andi?

They finished eating and headed back to the farm. When they pulled in the front gate, she grabbed his hand.

"Want to go down to the creek?"

Ross was more than willing to extend the evening, despite the fatigue that seemed to be his constant companion these days. Was it this particular assignment? Or just the job in particular? He couldn't stop thinking about the things Andi had said. It was like she'd given him permission to leave the Secret Service, and he'd never even considered it as an option.

He followed her directions along the edge of a pasture, down the hill to a small gravel turnaround, and parked. They walked through a small grove of trees and came to a little sand beach on the edge of the creek.

"I guess we should have stopped to grab chairs," Andi smiled as she sat down in the sand.

"I don't mind." For some reason, he didn't mind getting in the sand one bit at this beach, unlike the one in Florida. Of course, he knew why. He'd do just about anything to spend more time with Andi and unravel the tangle of contradictions and layers wrapped up within her.

She looked up at the sky and he followed her gaze to find the clearest night he could remember seeing. "Wow."

"Yeah. We don't get this back in Virginia, do we?"

"Not even close."

They watched the sky for a moment before Andi

broke the silence. "If you could leave your job and do anything, what would it be?"

His mind went to Candace. "I'm not sure." He had some ideas, crazy thoughts about what it would look like to be able to help people who needed it. But he wasn't ready to say them out loud. Even to Andi. "What about you?"

"I don't know. I like the idea of teaching self-defense. I tried to get Sensei Roberts to do it at Alexandria, but he thought a more complete practice was important. I guess I'm more practical than that. A woman doesn't need to know the entire philosophy of a martial art in order to know how to defend herself against a creep in a parking lot."

"That's really cool, Andi. I think women would really respond to you teaching them too."

She shrugged. "I don't know. Sometimes I have trouble connecting with people."

A smile tugged at the corner of his lips. "You don't say?"

She leaned her shoulder into his and nudged him.

He chuckled. "Don't say it like it's a bad thing. The fact that you don't let just anyone in makes it special for the ones you do. There is a genuineness to your interaction. I'd rather have a genuine connection that takes some effort than a false one that came easily."

Andi stared at the sky and he wondered if he had said something wrong. Finally she turned to him, her eyes shiny in the moonlight. "Thanks for that. I'm sorry if I shut you out at first."

"I forgive you. As long as you don't shut me out now." Then he leaned in to close the distance between them. The stars that filled the sky had nothing on the way Andi had taken up residence in his heart. Every dusty corner of his soul seemed illuminated by the fascinating, incredible woman sitting with him on the beach.

"Can you let me in, Dandelion?" he whispered, his lips an inch from her own.

ANDI FELT her heart jump at the sound of her name. Instead of the frustration and immediate recoil it usually brought, the sound of her full name on Ross's lips was liberating. She pressed into the kiss and hummed her approval when he responded in kind.

Since they met at the dojo all those months ago, Agent McClain had wriggled his way under her skin and into her heart. The invasion was completely unexpected and should have been completely unwelcome. Instead, though, Andi had discovered that perhaps she hadn't missed her chance at love. She'd just been waiting for the right person—and the right time. By every measure, Ross was the right person.

Was this the right time?

When they ended the kiss, he pressed his forehead against hers. "I don't want to say goodbye when this is over."

She shut her eyes against the unwelcome reminder.

The election was only a few weeks away, and they both knew what that meant. If Harrison was elected, it was entirely possible that Ross would be reassigned to his protection detail at the White House. If he wasn't, then he would be assigned to another unit, protecting someone else.

"I don't either," she answered truthfully. She blinked away the sting behind her eyes. She pulled back and shrugged. "And to think, I thought I wouldn't be able to get rid of you soon enough. Now, the idea of you leaving is unacceptable."

"Unacceptable, huh?" Ross looked like he liked that confession.

She nodded and crossed her arms, playing bossy. "Yep. I simply won't allow it. You can't leave."

"Sir, yes sir," he said with a smile before kissing her again. "Point of clarification?"

She put on her best Sergeant Major face. "Go ahead, soldier."

"What if you come with me?"

Andi's stern look transformed into a grin. "That might be an acceptable alternative. I'll have to check with my commanding officer."

She pointed up to the night sky and then dropped the amusing roleplay. "I think we both have a lot of things to pray about."

She certainly needed to pray about what was next for her. She'd been certain God told her that her time in the Army was up. But she hadn't really spent much time asking why before she'd marched forward with plans to move home.

Was she really prepared to leave home again for the chance to be with Ross? She'd never been the type to follow someone else. Unless that person wore the insignia of her CO. But if they were a team... Maybe it wasn't following. Maybe they were just moving in the same direction. Together.

15

When Jessica Street's name flashed on Ross's caller ID, his pulse skipped. She was Candace's best friend. And one of his by default. But he hadn't heard from her in years. Was there something new in Candace's case? His friends at the Police Department were supposed to call him if there were any new leads.

"McClain," he answered.

"Ross?"

He recognized Jessica's voice, but it wasn't the bubbly young woman he remembered. This voice was haggard and desperate.

"Jessica, what's wrong?"

"It's really bad, Ross. I didn't know who else to call. I'm in trouble."

"Whoa, whoa. It's okay. Tell me what's going on. Maybe I can help."

"I don't know. My boss is laundering money, and I found out. Now he's ticked and says they're going to kill me."

Ross's heart sank. What was he going to do? He was committed here, but the last thing he wanted was to leave Jessica defenseless the same way he had Candace.

"Okay, Jessica. Give me an hour and then I'll call you back. Can you find someplace safe for an hour?"

When they hung up, Ross immediately dialed another number.

"Come on, Ryder... pick up the phone." His brother's voicemail picked up and Ross left a quick message telling his brother to call back as soon as possible. Then he called his brother's roommate. Jessica wouldn't like this, but she didn't have another option.

"This is Flint." Flint Raven had been Ryder's best friend for over a decade, since they went to college together.

"Raven, this is Ross."

"Well, if it isn't Big Brother. What's up, man?"

"Where's Ryder?"

"I don't really know. You know how he is. I think

he took a job protecting some cargo headed for LA or something."

Ross shook his head. His brother had loads of potential. But when he'd lost his job as a police officer, he'd struggled to find direction. Which is why Ross had hoped he'd be free to help Jessica.

"What about you? You got some time?"

It didn't take long for Raven to agree. When he called Jessica back, he told her to go to his house and that someone would meet her there. Andi walked into the trailer and he held up a finger.

Just to be sure Jessica would actually show, he didn't drop the bomb that it was Flint waiting for her. He'd let the two of them cross that bridge when they came to it.

Andi gave him a questioning look when he hung up a few minutes later. "What was that all about?"

"A friend of mine is in trouble. I can't help her because I'm stuck here." He took a deep breath. "It's okay. I want to stay." Was he trying to convince Andi or himself? "I need to stay." He glanced at Andi and saw her worried face. "I found someone else to help protect her. He won't let anything happen to her."

Andi stood and wrapped her arms around him. "I'm glad she'll have someone. And I'm glad you're not leaving. Are you sure you're okay with it?"

202 | TARA GRACE ERICSON

His heart settled. "Yeah. Raven will keep me up to date about what's going on. That's enough." He kissed her forehead. "Thanks for understanding. Would you maybe pray with me for her though?"

"Of course."

He held her hands and prayed for his friend. He also prayed quickly for the decisions they both needed to make. This call from Jessica felt like another sign that maybe he had another purpose waiting for him if he left the Secret Service.

But how could he walk away from the career he'd built here in the service? He was finally being given leadership positions. And he really did enjoy his job —the logistics and the strategy. It was important work.

But if he didn't have the commitments here, he would have been able to help her himself. He had the resources and the expertise to help her face trouble of any sort. Flint was strong and smart, and definitely had resources—monetary ones that Ross didn't have. But he'd never been a bodyguard. Hopefully, that wouldn't end up being a problem when it came to protecting Jessie.

"Did you need something specific?"

"Can't I just come to say hi?"

He smiled. "Of course you can. I just wanted to make sure I didn't derail us too far."

"Well, that's good. Because I do actually have something. Captain Storm called me."

He raised an eyebrow. "I bet he did."

She rolled her eyes. "He said there was a fire at Coulter Ranch this afternoon. He's there now if we want to take a look."

"Let's go."

Coulter Ranch was only about ten minutes away, tucked between Minden and Terre Haute, south of Bloom's Farm. Ross's eyes widened at the ornate gated entry, complete with a large bronze cow statue. "Do you think that's what the idols look like in the Old Testament?"

Andi covered her mouth to stifle her laughter. "Stop it. We're working."

"I'm just saying. That's a big cow."

"From what I've heard, Mrs. Coulter is nice, but a little excessive in everything she does."

"And Mr. Coulter?" He couldn't hide his curiosity about what kind of couple had raised Harrison Coulter, who seemed incredibly kind and down-to-earth, despite his status.

"He's the polar opposite of his son," she replied plainly.

They didn't see Mrs. Coulter, but when they drove in and parked across from the fire engine, the governor's father was yelling into the phone out of hearing range. Ross would have loved to know what he was saying and whose fault he perceived this to be.

"He seems pleasant."

Andi pressed her lips together and was fighting back a smile. "He's... intense."

"I can see that. I can see how Coulter could harness some of that when he needs to, as well."

"Definitely. Did Daisy ever tell you about the time Harrison came and threw his weight around to help her out of a bind?"

Ross raised his eyebrows. "That doesn't sound very good from the outside."

Andi waved a hand. "It wasn't like that. There was a county building inspector harassing Daisy during the renovation. The way Daisy tells it, he was on a white horse and carrying a flaming sword, but you know how she is. Harrison—a state senator at the time—came by for a meeting and implied that the county might not be valuing small businesses like they should. The county commissioner investigated, and it turned out the inspector had a competing interest and didn't want Daisy to open the inn."

"I'm glad it worked out. I'll be majorly let down on my next job when I'm back to staying at the Bartlett Inn Express." The chain hotels were fine, but they definitely didn't have Bonnie Mae working in the kitchen.

Andi's smile didn't reach her eyes. It only took a moment, but when he realized what he'd said, he was kicking himself. There he went, mentioning leaving for another assignment. He reached for her arm. "Hey, even if I take another assignment—you know I want to come home to you, right?"

She shook her head. "Don't make promises you can't keep, McClain."

He tipped her chin up so she would look at him. "I don't," he said firmly.

Bryce walked over, his face shiny with sweat and smudged with ash.

"Hey, Bryce," Andi said. "Thanks for the call."

"Captain Storm, good to see you again."

"Come with me." Apparently, the captain wasn't in the mood for small talk today.

They followed him around the side of the large barn and suddenly the reason for the fire engine was obvious.

On the back side of the barn were the remnants of a tractor, a gaping hole in the fence, and a still-burning row of large hay bales. Ash covered the ground and smoke rose from the fire.

Andi spoke first. "You're not putting it out?"

Bryce shook his head. "That hay is gone. We're better off letting it burn and just controlling the fire so it doesn't spread."

Ross jumped in with a more important question. "What happened? I'm guessing since you called us, this wasn't spontaneous combustion?"

Bryce shook his head and pointed behind them. He and Andi turned, and he sighed at the familiar red writing.

You're dead meat.

"Well, then. That's reassuring." Andi's sarcasm mirrored his own thoughts. The activists were escalating. This fire was more dangerous—closer to the main house and larger in scale. He didn't know what it meant that they had targeted Coulter's family ranch, but he was sure the governor wouldn't respond positively.

"What else should we know?"

"Reggie Coulter is totally ticked. Whoever it was let about forty head of cattle escape through the broken fence before they lit the fire. He's trying to round them up, and he's arguing with the insurance agency because they want him to prove it wasn't his own negligence that led to the hay fire."

Ross nodded. "Got it. Our info should help with that. I'll go talk to him and try to calm him down." He turned to Andi. "Andi, take pictures and see if you can get anything on security or game cameras."

She raised an eyebrow, then saluted. He could practically feel the sarcasm in the gesture. "Yes, sir."

He turned and headed toward the governor's father before he let Captain Storm see him lose his composure at Andi's smart aleck response. Anyone other than the two of them would think nothing of it. He saw the undertones of the flirtation there, but this wasn't the time or place. They were working.

ANDI PULLED out her phone and headed toward the barn to grab pictures of the vandalism. No doubt Reginald Coulter would have it painted over by tomorrow. He liked to have everything in its place.

Bryce walked with her and Andi tried not to wrinkle her nose at the smell of smoke.

"So you and Agent Smith over there..."

She corrected him coolly. "Agent McClain?"

"Sure, whatever. You're... together?"

Andi stopped and turned to him. His steel-blue eyes were bright against the ashy remnants of the fire on his face. Bryce was a decent guy. Maybe in another life, they could have hit it off, but even twenty years ago, he'd been as rooted in Minden as the trees on Miss Ruth's property. That wasn't her. And even though she had moved back, there was something telling her that she wasn't meant to stay forever.

"Yeah. We are."

He rubbed a hand over his hair and sighed. "Figures."

"Sorry, Bryce. You'll find someone."

He tipped his head with a crooked smile. "Yeah, I guess. Good to see you, Andi. I hope we don't meet like this again," he joked.

"Me too. We're going to catch these guys."

As she said the words, Andi desperately prayed they were true. She wasn't as confident as she sounded. They needed a break in the case and this fire wasn't it.

Ross walked across the grass toward them, and Bryce waved at them both as he headed back to his crew.

"All good?" Ross asked as they watched the firefighter walk away, MRFD emblazoned across the back of his yellow coat.

"Yep. All good," she confirmed. "Do you need anything else here?"

He shook his head. "Let's head back. I've got an idea."

She pestered him in the car, but Ross wouldn't tell her his plan.

"I'm trying to think through it all. Just give me until we get there."

Andi sat back and crossed her arms. "Fine." Stubborn man. It wasn't as though they couldn't develop the plan together or anything. No, he had to do it himself, so her only option was either to look like the bad guy when she disagreed or to go along with it.

When they got back to the trailer, she whirled toward him the instant the door closed behind them.

"Now can you tell me?"

"Take a seat and I'll tell you the plan."

Andi pushed down her irritation at his bossiness. It didn't help her mood that he had an idea for the case when she didn't have anything.

He sat next to her at the corner of the table. "Here's my thought. I have no idea if the agency will go for it, but I want to work out the details before we check."

"Get on with it, McClain."

"Having the hanging threat of the activist group is worse for us than if we had any idea when they might strike next. So, what if we force their hand?"

He seemed energized by the idea, but Andi wasn't tracking. "Explain."

"What if there was an event on the governor's calendar that was irresistible for the Animal Liberation Alliance to crash?"

"You want to lure them out?"

He tipped his head from side to side. "Basically."

"Using Harrison as bait?" Andi's entire body went tense at the idea of hanging her brother-in-law out there as a trap for the ALA. "No way. That's crazy."

"Look, I know it's a bit unorthodox—"

"A bit?" Andi pushed back from the table and paced. "It's irresponsible and dangerous and I can't believe you of all people would suggest such a thing!"

She looked back at Ross. He was watching her pace, but not arguing with her.

"Aren't you going to say something?"

"Not yet. You're not ready to listen."

She narrowed her eyes at him, but she couldn't

argue. Why did he have to be right all the time? Andi took a deep breath. "Fine. I'm listening. But I still think it's a terrible idea." She sat back down. "Convince me why it's not."

"The first thing we need to remember is that Coulter is already out there, attending events and in potential danger right now. This would simply be a targeted way of forcing our friends to choose an event that we want them to. Which means we can prepare more effectively to protect him and apprehend them at the same time."

Andi nodded along. He made a bit of sense, as much as she hated to admit it.

"Poppy's going to say no."

"That's where you come in. Her first reaction is going to be the same as yours. Without the derogatory thoughts about me, I'd assume." Ross's spot-on evaluation of her inner dialogue made her smile sheepishly.

"I still don't like it. It feels too risky." She leaned toward him. "Do you really think your boss will go for it?" Andi felt uneasy about the whole idea, but she could see that no matter how much she argued with Ross, he was set on this idea. Stubborn man.

"I don't know. But I think it's our best chance to stop this before it goes too far in an unpredictable way. First, I think we need to talk to the governor and see if he is interested in a rally hosted by the Indiana Cattle Farmers Association."

"You really think they will just host an event with barely any notice?" She couldn't convince Ross to give up the idea, and if Secret Service somehow went along with it, she could only pray there was another roadblock in the plan.

"When they have the chance to get a former member and huge ally into the White House? Absolutely."

Darn. He was right. Who was going to turn down a chance to host an event for the local celebrity political candidate?

"Please, Ross. I don't have a good feeling about this."

"It's going to be okay, Andi. We will take every precaution to protect your brother-in-law It will just help us focus our efforts. We have to do this." Ross was every bit as adamant about the pros of the plan as she was about the cons.

What could she do? If she came out against the idea, Poppy would listen. But the last thing she wanted to do was go behind Ross's back. Why wouldn't the man just listen to her?

"If this crazy plan even happens—which I still

hope it doesn't—I want to be involved every step of the way," she demanded. If she couldn't stop the event, she was going to be darn sure that they didn't miss something. Her brother-in-law's life depended on it.

16

*R*oss tried to disappear into the woodwork as Andi stood up to sit closer to her sister, who was currently trying to burn him into ash with the fire in her eyes. He'd heard Daisy and Andi describe Poppy as feisty, but he had to admit that until now, he hadn't seen it. She was apparently very good at self-control.

"Are you crazy, Andi?" Mrs. Coulter whipped her head back and forth between them.

"Poppy, just listen."

"No, you listen! My husband is not hosting some event with the sole purpose of luring out some crazy person who thinks he deserves to be killed because his family raises beef cattle. It's absurd. Tell them, Harrison."

Andi was still trying to talk her sister down. "Please, Poppy. Just listen to the details." He admired the way Andi was backing his idea in front of the Coulters, even if she wasn't one hundred percent sold on the plan herself.

They felt like a team.

"I want to do it."

Mrs. Coulter's head snapped toward her husband. Her voice was quieter when she spoke. "What?" She sounded scared, and Ross's heart went out to her. The love between these two was palpable in every interaction.

"I said I want to do it. I'm sorry, Poppy. But the campaign trail is grueling as it is. This threat looming over me at every event has made it ten times worse. I'm convinced someone is going to douse me with a bucket of cow's blood at every rope line." The governor laid his hand on his wife's shoulder and she leaned into the contact. "I won't do it if you don't agree. But I'd like to try Agent McClain's plan."

There was a long moment of silence, with the exception of Mrs. Coulter's sniffles. Finally, she took a staggered breath and nodded. "Okay," she said quietly before turning her eyes to him. "Promise me you'll do everything you can to keep him safe."

"I swear to you."

The governor stood and shook his hand. "Thanks for everything. Let's get these people."

"Is there somewhere we can chat?" Ross's plan was to get Coulter to reach out to his contacts at the Cattle Farmers Association and get the ball rolling on a rally. Then he would get approval to add the event to the schedule, as though it were any other event. Once it was official, he would bring up the additional security concerns.

It felt a little duplicitous, but there was no reason for the Secret Service to veto this event if it was treated like any other. It just so happened to have been added to the schedule for two purposes. It really would be a good rally and fundraiser. And it would also be an irresistible target for the ALA to hit.

He ran through the details with Coulter.

"I don't love the fact that we are adding the event before everyone is on board with the added agenda. But I see why you're doing it."

Ross nodded. "Look, if for some reason the agency decides the event doesn't warrant extra security, we will cancel it. I don't think that will happen, because it is now so obvious what the perpetrators are trying to accomplish. But that's our backup plan.

Campaign events get canceled and rescheduled all the time."

Coulter nodded. "Sounds good. Give me a couple of dates and I'll reach out. We can host the event here to keep it simple."

Ross nodded. "My thought exactly. We already know the ALA is hanging out in the area. And hopefully having the event someplace they've already been successful at infiltrating will give them some confidence."

Coulter inhaled and gave an incredulous smile. "Seems crazy to hope that my attackers will feel emboldened."

"It's a bit counter-intuitive, isn't it?"

The governor sat in an armchair.

"Now that we've talked business, can I ask you about something else?"

Ross's brow wrinkled in confusion. "Sure. What's up?"

"You and Andi?"

"Ah." He was honestly surprised this was the first conversation he'd been ambushed with in this family. Well, Daisy couldn't stop dropping hints and suggestive smiles every time she saw him. But that was encouraging. This was... protective.

"Yeah. What's going on there?"

Ross smiled. "Look, Mr. Coulter, I respect you a great deal, and I am honored to be on your protection detail and that you trust me with this current situation. But I don't feel the need to answer your questions about my relationship with Andi. And I don't think she would particularly appreciate your interference either."

Coulter chuckled. "That's probably true." He held up his hands in surrender. "Fine, fine. But the fact that you called it a relationship, and that you talk about her as Andi and not as Miss Bloom is rather telling, Agent McClain. From what I can tell, you are a man who appreciates protocol. You aren't a rule breaker. Which has me wondering if somehow adding two rule followers together has resulted in a unit that doesn't seem to care quite as much."

Ross gave a slight smile. "Maybe you're right. I'm reconsidering a lot of things I've always considered to be important. And I'm reevaluating things I've written off as impossible for too long."

Coulter nodded knowingly. "I'll butt out, but I'll be the first to tell you that finding the right person changes everything. It sounds like you already realize that." He stood. "For what it's worth, you two seem good together."

"Thank you. You and your wife... I see a lot of political couples. You two have something special."

Coulter's face softened. "We really do. I hate to think where I would be without her. Or perhaps who I would be."

With that cryptic remark, Coulter walked out of the study, leaving Ross with no option but to follow him back to the living room. Andi and Poppy were laughing at something when he walked back in.

"Care to share with the class?" he joked.

"Not even a little," Andi replied. "Should we head back?"

"Yeah, let's go make some plans." He turned to Coulter. "When they get back to you with the date, let me know as soon as you can and we will get the ball rolling."

If everything went according to plan, The Animal Liberation Alliance will fall right into their trap. The FBI had provided what they knew about the ALA, but a membership roster wasn't one of them. He didn't know who they would be looking for at the event, but he'd know them when he saw them.

*a*ndi opened the door and let McClain in. She held her breath as she waited for his response.

"Whoa, this is nice."

She smiled nervously. "Thanks. The owner is working in the back, but I told him I wanted a friend to come check it out with me before I bought it."

He looked around. "So, you really want to buy your own dojo?"

She shrugged. "It seems like the right thing to do, you know? I like teaching. I'm back here, and let's be honest—my job at the farm isn't much of a job once the campaign is over." Once they caught the members of the ALA that were after Harrison, it would be back to normal.

And Ross would leave.

Ross wandered through the dimly lit dojo. "Sure. It makes sense."

She nodded. It *did* make sense. She'd always been logical, and opening a dojo was a measured, rational next step for her future.

The lack of excitement she felt didn't mean it was the wrong choice. It just meant it was a safe choice, right?

Safe was good. She liked safe.

"Why is he selling?"

His question pulled her from her thoughts. "What?"

"Why is the sensei selling this place? Is it a money pit?"

She smiled. "I don't think so. Sounds like he just wants to spend more time with his grandkids."

"Ah." Ross gave a couple of well-aimed kicks at the center of a martial arts dummy. "Does it come with all the equipment and everything?"

She nodded. "It does. That was one thing I liked about it. I looked at a couple other spaces, but the idea of starting from the ground up was daunting."

"I never thought you were one to back down from a challenge."

Ross's tone made her frown. He wasn't exactly being supportive.

They walked along the edge of the mat.

"What do you think?" She was dying to know his thoughts. They held a lot of weight, despite their uncertain future.

"It's a nice space. I'm sure you'll be great at it."

There was something in his voice though. "But?"

He turned toward her and gestured to the empty space. "Is this what you want?"

"I'm not sure."

He looked deeply into her eyes until she squirmed. She held her tongue though. Seeming to realize he wouldn't get any more of an answer than that, Ross slipped off his shoes and walked to the center of the mat.

He held a hand out to her and cupped it in a 'come and get me' motion.

"Come on. Let's dance."

With a smile, Andi slipped out of her shoes and stepped onto the mat as she shrugged out of her jacket.

She stood opposite him in the center of the mat. Ross pressed his fist into his palm near his chest and bowed. Andi responded in kind.

Neither of them had pads, so it would be a light

contact sparring match. At half speed, Andi lunged with her right hand first. He met her attack easily, deflecting it with his forearm and countering with a low kick from her left.

Back and forth they went, slowly trading punches and blocks. When he caught her fist in his hand, she attacked with the other. He caught it as well and then brought her arms down to her waist as they both laughed. The motion pulled her close, face to face with him. Despite the easy pace of their exercise, her pulse was elevated and her breathing was labored.

Their smiles died and Andi stared into Ross's blue eyes. She lifted onto her toes and pressed a kiss to his lips. His grip loosened on her hands and one hand came around her waist. Her body pressed against his, and she savored the way his kiss made her feel. For a woman who always took control—demanded it most of the time, Ross's kiss made her feel deliciously out of control.

Reckless even.

There were few things she had ever enjoyed as much as sparring—verbally and otherwise—with Ross McClain. Kissing him was definitely one of those things.

She smiled with a devious thought. Right now,

she could tell Ross had completely forgotten about their sparring match.

She adjusted slowly, repositioning her feet. Then she broke the kiss. Quickly, she dropped to the floor and swept her leg under his feet.

"What—"

His question was cut off as he lost his balance and landed on the floor next to her. Andi laughed at his incredulous expression.

Ross rolled over onto his back with a groan. "You're going to pay for that."

"Sure."

"As soon as I can move again."

"Whatever you say, old man."

"Oh, come on. I'm only a couple of years older than you. Besides, you tricked me." He leaned up on his elbows.

"Did I?"

He smiled. "Mm-hmm. I think it's a violation of the rules of engagement to distract your opponent like that."

"Oh? Were you distracted?" Andi couldn't help but smile and tease him.

"Very."

She scooted across the floor and leaned down to meet him eye to eye. "I would say I'm sorry, but that would be a lie."

In a flash, Andi was on her back. Ross had reversed their positions and was now hovering over her, his legs off to the side.

"You were saying something?"

She nodded, unable to speak.

He turned his head so she saw his ear. "Sorry, I couldn't hear you. Did you have something to say?"

She laughed and shook her head, pressing her lips together.

He grinned. "Surrender!"

"Never," she responded stubbornly.

Ross sighed. His eyes dropped to her lips, then back to her face. "You drive me crazy, Andi." Then he rolled away from her, settling on his back. They stared at the ceiling together.

"So, you really want to open a gym?"

It was the third time he'd asked, but she still wasn't sure how to answer.

"Yes." Even as she said it, she could hear the lie on her lips. "No." But that didn't sound right either. "I just want to do something. I've been working for twenty years being a cog in a huge machine. And don't get me wrong, I loved what I did, and I loved knowing that I played a small part in some huge operations. But I want to know what it's like to be the boss in a small machine. It's never been just me."

As independent as she was, there was the unanswered question: could she do it on her own? Whatever *it* was.

The question of *if* was every bit as unnerving as the question of *what*.

Ross was quiet. "That makes sense. It just... sounds lonely, doesn't it? Ever think there might be room for two in the driver's seat?"

She turned her head toward him. "What are you saying?"

"I don't know. I've been thinking a lot about what I want to do too. I just can't figure out if this is the end of my time at the Secret Service."

His words made her heart jump. Was he really considering leaving? What would that mean for them?

She grinned as she stared at the ceiling again. "Ever think about opening a dojo?"

There was a smile in his voice when he responded. "Not even a little bit."

"What do you want to do?"

"Honestly? I've been spinning around this crazy idea about a security firm." Saying the words out loud felt really good. Like it became a real possibility because he had physically acknowledged the option existed. "This whole mess with my friend Jessica brought it all up again. I hate that I wasn't there to help take care of her. It was like Candace all over again."

Her heart broke at the sorrow in his voice.

He continued, his voice stronger. "At least Raven was able to take care of it. I've got money. A friend who might be able to help start things up. We could take some paying contracts to keep the lights on, but mostly just try to help people who can't help themselves. But," he paused and she turned her head to meet his eyes, "I think I'd like a partner. Maybe someone who specializes in logistics and hand-to-hand combat?"

Andi flushed with pleasure at the compliment. He wanted to partner with her? A security firm?

"I... I don't know what to say."

"Maybe just think about it. I've been turning this around in my head for a week or two, and the more I think about it, the more I like it. But if you aren't on board, then maybe it isn't meant to be. I didn't realize you were so set on a dojo."

She blurted out, "I'm not!"

He chuckled. "I'm not trying to talk you out of it!

You can do it if you want to. But I just thought this might be another option."

"It's a good option. I never considered it." She leaned up on one elbow and looked down at him. "Let me think and pray about it. It already feels really good." She looked around the dojo. "Maybe I've just been so busy grasping for anything at all that I didn't realize what I grabbed wasn't the right fit." She met his eyes. "When it's right, you can feel it."

Ross leaned up on his elbow to mirror her position. "Yeah, you really can."

He reached forward and tucked his hand under her ear, cradling her jaw. Ever so gently, he pulled her closer. "You and I? We feel right. Everything else will fall into place. Dojo or security firm or something else entirely. Dandelion Bloom, we could run a restaurant together if you said that was your dream."

She smiled. "Can you cook?"

"I make a mean mac and cheese." His tone was light, but his eyes were focused on hers. "I love you, Andi. And I'm on board with whatever comes next."

Ross LOOKED around the conference room at his team. The event was tomorrow, and everyone was on high alert. Already, there were ten extra agents lining the walls. More would arrive today and in the morning.

He'd already run through the logistics of the event, confirming assignments for each agent.

"Any questions?" No one spoke, so he dismissed the group with a simple, "Thanks, everyone. Ridgeway, can I talk to you? You too, Bloom."

Andi's eyebrows arched when he added her name to the request. After the room had cleared, he waved the three of them into his office.

"What's up, boss?" Agent Ridgeway was clearly curious about the extra discussion.

He took a deep breath and prayed for wisdom. "I probably shouldn't be telling you both this, but I need to. There have been suspicions of a leak on our team. We think they've been involved in several incidents over the last year."

Ridgeway swore and Ross gave her a pointed look. "My thoughts are similar, though perhaps not as colorful."

"Who is it?"

Ross shook his head. "I'm not sure yet. And they haven't done anything since we've been on Governor Coulter's protection. I don't expect this to cause any problems tomorrow, but I needed you to be eyes open."

Andi's eyes widened. "We can't go through with tomorrow if your team has a leak! It's asking for something terrible to happen, Ross."

Ridgeway clucked her tongue. "I have to agree with the civilian, sir."

His jaw clenched. Why were they teaming up against him?

"I've talked this over with Gallo and we still feel like this is the best course of action."

Andi crossed her arms. "So our opinions don't matter?"

He bristled against the comment. "Of course they do. But in this moment, I'm telling you—as the team leader for this detail—that we are moving forward and that I've got everything under control."

He could see Andi bite down her objection with a curt nod and pressed lips. The unwilling acceptance in her expression bordered on anger. He wondered how many times she'd been forced to swallow orders she didn't agree with.

Ross didn't want to play the heavy-handed commander. But they were too close to the ALA to give up now. All signs indicated they would try something at the event tomorrow. And he was going to make sure they caught them. Nobody—not Andi, Ridgeway, or even the leak—was going to stop him.

He wouldn't be able to look himself in the mirror if he let anything happen to Harrison Coulter. Even worse, perhaps—he wouldn't be able to look at Andi.

18

*T*he next day at the Indiana Cattle Farmer's Association Rally, Andi could feel the anticipation in her body. Every muscle was on edge, ready to pounce.

If only she knew who the target was. She'd looked at the blurry photo of the woman in the woods so many times, it was seared into her brain. Would she recognize the woman if she saw her? Or would they even send the same person? Dealing with an organization meant it could be anyone.

The stage had been setup inside Storybook Barn, and all the tables had been removed. Instead, there were rows of chairs with standing room in the back.

The morning sun had barely crested the hill in the east, but the barn was a flurry of activity as

Secret Service agents and local law enforcement prepared for the noontime event. Andi paced the edge of the room outside the door that led to her and Lily's offices.

"Coffee?" Ross's voice made her jump. She turned to find him with an extended hand and a disposable cup.

She shook her head. "No thanks. I'm already wired. Caffeine would just put me over the edge, I'm afraid."

"Fair enough." He stepped closer, and they faced the ballroom together. "Are you nervous?"

Andi shrugged a shoulder. Nervous didn't seem like entirely the right word. "A little. Eager, maybe? I'm ready to get this over with."

"I know what you mean. I'll still have the remainder of the detail to finish, but it feels like this event is the biggest obstacle between now and... whatever comes next."

Her mind couldn't help but wander back to those same words whispered on the sparring mat of the dojo she wasn't buying. Whatever comes next.

She reached for his hand. "Thanks for being here for Harrison. I'm glad it was you and your team. Even if I haven't agreed every step of the way, I really do trust your decisions." That was hard to admit. Andi was still on edge about today, but even though she'd made her objections known—this was happening. She was praying and trusting.

Ross smiled warmly. "That means a lot. I know you weren't exactly happy to see me when I showed up on the farm."

"I wasn't unhappy. More like... surprised."

He chuckled. "That's not how I remember it."

"Well then, you need your memory checked," she teased. "Because I was nothing but gracious."

He grinned and sipped his coffee. "No comment." There was a beat of silence as they both studied the orchestrated chaos in front of them. He turned toward her before continuing quietly. "Today is going to go fine. We have no reason to think the activists will try anything especially violent, despite their tough talk in the messages. My friends at the FBI think the profile is consistent with perpetrators more interested in gaining attention and making a splash than actually hurting someone."

Andi nodded. He'd told her the same thing before. It was a good reminder though. "We can handle a bunch of over-zealous vegetarians, but it would be nice if they were toting picket signs instead of pipe bombs."

"Speaking of pipe bombs..." Ross waved to a man

with one of the working dogs and he came over. "Hey, Frank. Glad you're here. Who is this handsome guy?"

The man looked down at the German Shepherd at his side. "This is Roscoe. Just got him a few weeks ago from DK9 out in Colorado. Best dog I've worked with in a long time."

"Thanks for bringing him out here from Indianapolis. It's hard to secure a property this large, so we just want to make sure nothing managed to sneak in while we weren't looking. Can you take Roscoe and sweep the barn and the bed-and-breakfast? Then we'll have you working the front gate while people are coming in as well."

"You got it." The man led Roscoe back out of the barn.

She turned her head and raised her eyebrows. "Bomb-sniffing dogs?"

"Standard protocol," he responded.

Andi pushed down her irritation at his nonchalant answer. This was his rodeo, and he knew what he was doing. The dogs were no big deal. It didn't mean they expected a bomb. She knew this wasn't like her tours overseas, where the dogs sometimes sacrificed their lives finding the explosives before they made it onto base.

A few minutes later, someone called for Ross. "I better go handle this." He reached out and squeezed her hand. "I'll see you after the event, okay?"

She nodded. "Yes, sir." Despite her lighthearted response, she couldn't fight the gripping pressure building in her chest. Anxiety.

Andi took a deep breath and pushed it back down until the tightness in her chest eased. It would all be over soon.

Ridgeway jogged up to her. "Hey, we need you. Blueberry is a bit nervous." Ridgeway used the Secret Service codename for Poppy. "Actually, more than a bit. She's close to losing it."

"I'm on my way."

Andi found her sister at the bed-and-breakfast, pacing the sitting room. The kids were safely tucked away with their grandparents at the main house.

"Oh, thank heavens you're here. Tell me I'm crazy. Tell me it's all going to be okay."

She reached for her sister's hands. "Take a deep breath, Poppy."

Gently, she led her to the couch and continued slow, measured breathing.

Poppy hung her head. "Thank you."

Andi squeezed her fingers. "It's okay. You're not crazy. Here, let's pray together."

She prayed and poured her heart out to the Lord. "Keep Harrison and Poppy safe today. Help us catch those who threaten them. Calm these anxious thoughts and guide our steps. We are trusting you, God. Where we clamor for control, we are handing it over to you."

That was the prayer she needed to pray. Not just for this event, but for her entire life. Where she was scrambling for direction and domain and to control every little thing—she needed to hand it over to God.

After they finished praying, Andi left Poppy to make some calls and headed back to Storybook Barn.

When the event started, Andi held her position outside the office door. It was a low-level assignment, which kind of stung, but also gave her plenty of opportunity to watch the event unfold and keep her eyes open for anything unusual.

Poppy was with Harrison as he worked the room, playing the perfect campaign wife. Harrison made his way up the steps to the stage and gave a quick kiss to Poppy as she took her position just behind him to the left. Andi's eyes shifted away from them to the crowd.

The attendees seemed to be a predictable demographic. In a sea of mostly overweight, balding middle-aged men, Ross stood out in his suit. He hadn't had cause to wear it too much around the farm and Andi had to admit she didn't mind the whole black-tie bodyguard look at all.

She was busy watching him when she saw his hand fly to his ear and his eyes widen in fear. At the same time, she heard the shout.

"Gun!"

19

*T*ime stood still as Ross turned away from the main door he was watching and turned toward the audience behind him. The agents stationed in the hayloft had been watching a few people who seemed out of place. Nothing too suspicious. But then they'd uttered the words he heard in his nightmares.

There's a gun.

As he took in the scene, Agent Ridgeway and the rest of the floor team were already in motion—a blur of black flashing through the crowd and crashing on the location.

He heard the loud crack of a gunshot and registered two agents on stage, covering Coulter with their bodies and quickly ushering the governor off the stage and out the side exit.

Updates came through his earpiece in succinct sentences.

"Buckeye and Blueberry secure, leaving the premises."

"Two subjects apprehended."

He issued commands into his radio. "Lock it down. Nobody gets out."

He saw Andi's face, the questions burning in her eyes. He'd let her down, and the failure was threatening to choke him. She would have every right to hate him after this.

Right now, he needed to focus one hundred percent on securing the scene, protecting the governor and his agents. As much as he ached to go to her, Andi would just have to wait.

He spoke as he walked past her. "I'm sorry. I've got to take care of this first. I promise, I'll find you as soon as I can."

Her quiet nod of understanding was full of hurt and confusion, but he ignored it and kept moving.

How had this happened?

Then he spoke into the radio to his team again. "Somebody figure out how they got a gun in here! And get me an interrogation room."

ANDI'S HEART had dropped to her stomach when she heard the gunshot. This wasn't supposed to happen. More than anything, she wished she had been granted one of the stupid radios the Secret Service was using to communicate. The barn looked like chaos. Harrison and Poppy were disappearing out the back. Had either of them been hit? Where was the shooter?

She had found Ross's eyes and waited for information from him—any scrap of intel that would let her know everything was okay. What had gone wrong with the plan? There weren't supposed to be guns. Ross had said they wouldn't get violent.

But Ross hadn't stopped.

And he hadn't listened to her. If he'd just listened to her objections, this wouldn't have happened.

The helpless feeling rose higher within her. She hated feeling out of control. In some ways, she'd designed her whole life to avoid that feeling. It's why she practiced martial arts. It's why she'd joined the Army. And yet, here she was—her family's life on the line and she couldn't do anything.

Activity swirled around her, and anxiety ratcheted up within her. She pressed her eyes closed against the torrent of emotion.

When she opened her eyes, the blur of activity wasn't quite so overwhelming. She saw Agent Ridgeway talking down the crowd near the exit. Her cheek was bleeding slightly, and she looked spent.

Andi went over. "Hey. What do you need from me?"

Ridgeway's grateful look gave Andi purpose. "Can you make an announcement or something? We need everyone to stay put, but you can tell them that the governor is fine and the shooter has been apprehended."

"What about Poppy?"

"They're both fine."

"Thank you. I've got this. You go take care of that cut." Andi made her way to the stage and did just that. She directed everyone to the bottled water available around the room and promised everyone it would get sorted out soon.

When she stepped down off the stage, Ross was waiting for her.

"Thanks. We needed someone to do that."

"Yeah, Ridgeway asked. Is everyone okay?"

She tried not to, but Andi knew she was being cold with him. Not only had he not listened to her before the event, it had hurt more than she wanted to admit that he had brushed her off in the heat of the moment.

"Everyone is good. Shot went high and no one was hit. Ridgeway took an elbow to the face during the takedown, but otherwise no one was hurt, praise the Lord."

Andi nodded. She was glad everyone was okay, but she couldn't deny how angry she felt at Ross right now.

He ducked down to meet her gaze. "Are we okay?"

She looked over his shoulder instead of meeting his eyes as she tried to find the words. "You said this wouldn't happen." Then she looked at him and spoke softer. "You didn't listen to me."

Ross's eyes closed, and he pressed his lips together. "I'm so sorry, Andi. I really thought I was doing the best thing."

"Maybe that's the problem. You're always so sure you know what the best thing is that it doesn't occur to you that there is another option. That someone else might have ideas worth listening to!"

"I know you're upset, Andi." He laid a hand on her shoulder, but she jerked away.

"This was my family, Ross."

Sadness filled his eyes. "I know, and I'm sorry. I never meant for this to happen. Everyone is okay, and we have the shooter in custody. Our plan worked, even if it was a bit out of our control."

"*Your* plan. Not ours. You talk about being a team, but when the rubber meets the road—you had to do it yourself."

With that, Andi turned and walked away. She needed to get eyes on her sister and Harrison. Ross would just have to wait if he wanted to hash this out again.

Ross watched Andi walk away, waiting for her to turn back and admitting that he knew she wouldn't. She held him responsible, and he couldn't blame her. It had been his plan.

Like usual, he'd stormed ahead with his vision of the solution. And look where it had gotten them. It could have been so much worse. He considered them lucky that no one had gotten seriously hurt.

Andi was right to blame him. He blamed himself.

The best thing he could do now was make sure they got to the root of the threats against Coulter. He was pretty sure the man and woman they'd apprehended weren't the brains of the operation.

Fifteen minutes later, the curly-haired woman sat meekly across the table from him.

"What do you mean the gun was waiting for you?"

Apparently, the reality of Tiffany's situation was beginning to sink in. "We just wanted to teach them all a lesson. Willow said that the only way to get them to stop killing innocent animals was to kill one of them."

Ross held back his emotion at the horrifying logic in that statement. "And Willow is...?"

"She's my friend. She started the ALA, you know?" The admiration in the young woman's eyes was sickening. It was starting to sound like the ALA was more of a cult than anything else.

"Tell me more about how you got the weapon."

"I already told you. It was waiting for us. Willow said it would be. That she had someone on the inside."

McClain clenched his jaw. "Do you know who? Somebody local?"

The girl shook her head. "I don't think so. It cost her a lot of money. We all had to contribute so she could pay her rent this month, since the man was so expensive."

She knew it was a man. Maybe she knew more than she realized.

"So Willow paid this man to leave a gun for you at the barn."

Tiffany nodded. "I guess so."

"Did you ever meet him?"

She shook her head. "Willow just called him the Man in Black."

With that piece of information, Tiffany locked in the final piece of the puzzle. He left her in the small office and headed back into the main room of the barn.

Claussen was chatting with Ridgeway, who was holding an icepack to her cheek.

It took everything inside him to ask calmly, "Got a minute?"

He took Claussen into the small sound booth in the back of the barn.

"I've been trying to figure out how these guys got a gun in here. We wanded everyone at the door. We had dogs at entrances, and they swept the place this morning."

Claussen shook his head. "I don't know, man.

Maybe they just got one past the guys at the door? Or maybe one of the locals let them in?"

He was a good liar, Ross would give him that.

"That's an interesting theory. But I've got another one."

Claussen waited with a disinterested stare.

Ross felt his irritation rise. "Here's what I think. I think there's a Secret Service agent out there selling his loyalty to the highest bidder. Turning a blind eye so a known criminal can sneak into a restricted event, or stashing a gun in a secure area for someone to retrieve later."

Claussen's face fell. "How'd you know?"

"They called you the Man in Black."

"Whatever, McClain. Not everyone is happy making pennies their whole life, protecting people who don't appreciate it. Who make more money in a year than I will make in my entire life as their human shield. What makes their life more valuable than mine? Huh?"

Ross shook his head in disgust. "You've got it all wrong, Claussen. No one's life is worth more. But everyone's life is worth saving." He grabbed his former friend's arm and twisted it behind his back, pushing him out of the booth after relieving him of his weapon. He waved down one of the state police troopers and had Claussen handcuffed.

It was nice to put the mystery to bed of what had happened in Denver, but he wished it had been a different explanation. He wished a lot of things could be different—including the way things stood with Andi.

20

*A*ndi checked in with the agents posted at Poppy's house. The perimeter patrol she could see was already far more than the single agent who usually guarded the door.

She rushed up the front steps and into the waiting arms of her sister.

Immediately, Andi started talking. "I'm so sorry, Poppy! Are you okay?"

"Whoa, whoa. We're okay."

Andi stepped back. "Let me look at you."

She surveyed her sister. Her hair was slightly mussed, but otherwise Poppy seemed fine.

"Are you sure you're not hurt?"

Poppy led her inside. "I promise. We're okay."

Andi shook her head. "I'm so sorry, Poppy. This

wasn't supposed to happen. Ross said they weren't violent but—" Her voiced cracked painfully. "I never should have listened to him. I let my feelings for him cloud my judgement. But not anymore."

She would never forgive herself for not pushing harder.

"Shhh, Andi. It's okay. Really. It all worked out. Agent Rogers says they have the people in custody. Maybe this was the way it had to happen."

"I don't believe that. There had to be another way. One where you weren't in danger."

Poppy put her hands on Andi's shoulders. "Look at me. We're okay. We don't blame you, Andi. Harrison and I always knew this was a risk. But we also know that God is in control—no matter what."

Her mind went back to her conversation with her sister before the event. Here she was, clamoring for control again, when what she needed to do was trust that God had it covered.

Too many times, she tried to wrench control from the grasp of her Creator. What a fruitless struggle that would always turn out to be.

She took a deep breath and said a quick prayer for peace. It was time to admit that she wasn't in control.

And neither was Ross.

They could never really be in control, no matter how much they wanted to be. Which meant she couldn't blame Ross for choosing the path he genuinely thought was best. She knew him well enough to know he hadn't taken the risk lightly.

She hugged her sister tightly. "Thanks, sis. I love you so much."

"I love you, too. Now go. And tell Agent McClain we don't blame him either."

Ross LOOKED up from the blue light of the computer at his desk. When had it gotten dark?

His eyes widened at the sight of Andi in the doorway. He tried to read the expression on her face. Was she coming to say goodbye for good? Or to dress him down for his failure?

Maybe both.

"How's your sister?" Andi raised her eyebrows and he shrugged. "My team told me you were there."

"She's okay." Andi stepped into the office and he rolled back from the desk to make room for them to talk. "She said to tell you they don't blame you."

He nodded. Mrs. Coulter proved, yet again, to be full of grace. But right now, he wasn't especially concerned about what she thought. He was preoccupied with the opinion of a different Bloom sister. "Do you blame me?"

"I did."

He waited, his hopes hanging on whatever came next. Could she forgive him?

"Then Poppy helped me remember that I wasn't in control."

He frowned. If it hadn't been for him, she would have been in control.

"She reminded me that God was in control of the situation. As much as I want to micromanage everything, it's not mine to orchestrate. And it's not yours either. You did what you thought was best. And sure, I would have liked you to consider my objections a bit more, but I know you took the threat seriously. How can I blame you for doing what you felt was right?" She met his stare. "Sometimes it's hard for me to give up control. To God—or anyone else."

The hint of a smile teased at his lips. "I have a feeling you aren't alone in that struggle. In fact, I think I know a guy with the same problem."

She looked up at him and he saw the uncertainty in her eyes. "Maybe we can work on it together."

"That does sound like a good team mission." He stood to wrap her in his arms. "I'm so sorry it happened the way it did. I'm sorry I steamrolled your objections. But you have no idea how glad I am that Poppy said whatever she said to you."

Andi laughed. "Me too."

With that, he pressed his lips to hers, delighted at the way she pressed into him. At the end of one of the longest days of his career, there was nowhere he'd rather be than holding Dandelion in his arms. He kissed her thoroughly, apologizing again—this time without words.

He'd made his share of mistakes, though perhaps none so costly as this one could have been. Ross had forgotten the same thing Andi had mentioned. His pride and his own need for control had almost ended with disaster.

The kiss ended on a sweet sigh, and Ross held her tightly for a moment longer. Maybe he wasn't in control of everything, but he wasn't letting this moment end quite yet. If it were up to him, he would let it carry over and echo into the rest of their lives.

"Do you need anything from me?" Andi's quiet question brought him out of his dreaming of the future. He still needed to sort out the aftermath of the day and prepare the team for the rest of the campaign. There was still another month until election night.

254 | TARA GRACE ERICSON

He shook his head. "We got this. I think the most important thing is for you to be there for your family."

"Okay. But I'm here for you, too—if you need me."

"I do need you, love. More than I care to admit sometimes." Ross was starting to realize that Dandelion was true to her namesake flower. Except she wasn't unwanted and invasive. She was tenacious and resilient.

And beautiful in her own right.

21

*A*ndi couldn't ever remember an election night being so stressful. She'd paid attention to politics over the years. It was always a good idea to be informed about the person who was her commander-in-chief. But never had she watched the results come in with such interest. Storybook Barn had been transformed into a sea of red, white, and blue. A large projection screen was hung on one wall, with network news being broadcast on silent.

Harrison's family, friends, and biggest supporters ate and talked and cheered as results rolled in. With each state's results, the anchors kept track of what was needed to clinch the White House.

A hand came around the waist of her black dress,

and she relaxed into Ross's strong frame. "Hey, you. Aren't you working?"

He shook his head. "Nope. As of midnight tonight, I am officially retired as a Secret Service agent of the United States."

She grinned. "Retired sounds awfully old, doesn't it?"

He chuckled. "It really does. But you retired before me... so what does that say about you?"

She turned toward him and wrapped her arms around him, tipping her face up. "Probably that I'm quicker on the take."

"That's probably true. I can be a little slow to see what's right in front of my face."

"And what do you see now?"

"I see a beautiful woman who needs to be kissed —and a future that stretches before both of us, full of possibilities."

Andi's heart sang as he lowered his face to hers and kissed her. His lips were soft and warm, and she tightened her grip. His face was smooth, and the scent of his aftershave filled her senses. She moved her hands around to run down the front of the black suit and tie. Cheers rose from the crowd around them, and Andi pulled back in embarrassment, only to realize they were cheering because the results of another state had been finalized, bringing Harrison and Senator Waters one step closer to being named the winner.

"You know, I'm really going to miss this suit, I think."

He laughed. "I'll keep it around. Might need it if I run in the same circles as the vice president. Besides, if it gets you to wear that little black dress again, I'll gladly pull out the monkey suit."

She blushed. Andi loved her cargo pants and t-shirts, but there was something about getting dressed up and slipping into high heels that made her feel powerful too. Knowing that Ross approved wasn't a bad thing either.

Late in the evening, Harrison's campaign manager turned the volume up.

"Hush, hush! Everybody listen up. They're making an announcement!"

Andi and Ross watched, arm in arm, as Senator Waters and Governor Harrison Coulter were announced as the winner of the presidential election.

Andi screamed and hugged Ross. "Oh my goodness. They did it!"

When they finally got the chance to talk to

Harrison in the sea of well-wishers, Ross held out his hand. "Congratulations, Mr. Vice President."

Harrison smiled broadly. "Think it'll get old by the time four years go by?" They all laughed, and he continued. "Agent McClain, thank you for everything you did during this campaign. I don't know if I really get a say in things like this, but I'd be honored if you would continue as the lead of our protective detail moving forward."

Andi watched as Ross smiled. "I appreciate the offer, but I have something else in mind." Ross tugged her closer to his side. "Andi and I are starting our next adventure together. We're not sure what it will turn into yet, but Black Tower Security is going to make a positive difference in the world. For now, that's going to be enough."

Andi was suddenly wrapped in the arms of her sister. "I'm proud of you, sis," Poppy whispered.

"Me? You're the Second Lady!" Andi said with a laugh. "I'll never forget when you called me for advice about Harrison and his proposal. If you'd have said it would end up in the White House, I would have called you crazy."

"I'm pretty sure you did call me crazy," Poppy said with a wink.

"Yeah, well... it kind of was. But God worked it out, didn't He?"

"He'll do the same for you, if you let him." Poppy replied.

Andi turned and looked at Ross next to her. "I'm pretty sure He already has."

EPILOGUE

*H*awthorne poked his head into the study of the small craftsman-style home.

"You almost ready?"

Avery looked up at him, her fingers on the keyboard. "Sorry! The deadline for this conference is tonight, and I just know I won't want to do it after dinner. I'll be in a food coma."

He chuckled. "Take your time. Dinner is at two. We'll be just fine."

There was little more attractive to Hawthorne than Avery and her dedication to her work. Thanksgiving Day and she was hard at it.

Of course, he could relate. He'd spent the morning making sure the animals were fed and watered, since Lindsay went home to be with her family for the holiday. He never would have guessed how much he would enjoy managing Bloom's Farm. For all the year's he had resisted the job, he couldn't imagine doing anything else now.

A few minutes later, Avery rushed out of the study. "I'm ready, I'm ready."

Hawthorne held out a hand and pulled her close. "I love you."

She took a deep breath and leaned into his chest. "And I love you."

"You sure you don't mind staying here for Thanksgiving again? We haven't been out to see your parents since last year."

Avery smiled. "It's okay. I love Christmas in Freedom. They don't mind either. Maybe if we were holding grandkids hostage, they'd be more insistent. My sister says they hound her to bring the kids over constantly."

He squeezed her tightly. They'd discussed having kids at length, but both agreed it wasn't what they wanted. With nearly a dozen nieces and nephews, they had plenty of future generations to invest in—on short-term assignments.

"I know my family is excited to have everyone

together for one last time before Poppy and Harrison move to DC."

"I still can't believe my brother-in-law is going to be the vice president."

"You're telling me! I've seen Poppy covered in manure after fertilizing the fields. Now I see her on the evening news. It's just quite a change from ten years ago."

Avery gave him a warm smile. "She'd probably say the same thing. I know I would. What's it been. About ten years since I ran into you and your friends in the bar?"

Hawthorne groaned. "I thought maybe you'd forgotten about that."

"I hope I never do! It helps me appreciate the man you are today. Hawthorne Bloom, I'm so proud of you."

His heart swelled, and he pressed a kiss to her forehead. "Thanks, babe. I know God changed me back then, but I know I wouldn't have let him do it until you came into the picture."

Hawthorne would always be grateful God had reached into his broken life and redeemed it for something better. He didn't have to be afraid of failure, because God and Avery accepted him just as he was.

DAISY RESISTED the urge to shoo the last guests out of the bed-and-breakfast. Other than Ross, who was staying there for the holiday, she'd closed for Thanksgiving weekend. She didn't want any distractions as they enjoyed one last holiday before Andi moved back to Virginia and Poppy and Harrison moved to DC.

It didn't hurt that she could really use the time to rest. The first trimester had been hard when she was expecting Brielle, but chasing the two-year-old around along with nausea and exhaustion was a whole new ball game. Not to mention the almost-forty part of the equation.

Lance opened the door and held it open as Bonnie Mae waved and headed out. "See you next week!"

"Happy Thanksgiving, Bonnie."

"You too, sugar."

Lance shut the door behind Bonnie and came over to the small rolltop desk where she was working. "You almost ready?"

He rubbed her shoulders lightly and Daisy almost moaned.

"Just waiting for the Perkins to check out." A

yawn escaped as she continued, "Another twenty minutes, tops. And I need to find Bonnie's check. I printed it the other day, but now..."

"Why don't you go grab a nap in the sunroom? I'll check them out and then wake you up." There he went, being all thoughtful and stuff.

"Are you sure? Where's Bri?"

"I already dropped her at your parents' house. She's helping Grandma wash potatoes."

"But Bonnie's check—"

"I'll find it. Your desk is due for a cleanup anyway," he said with a grin.

She eyed the messy stacks of paper. Old habits died hard. Daisy smiled. "Okay then. You don't have to tell me twice. I won't sleep, but I'll just lie down for a bit."

She stood and stretched before turning and hugging her husband of five years. "You know I love you, right?"

He winked. "That's just because I give you Dr. Pepper and keep your business receipts organized."

She chuckled. "Well, I have to admit that is very sexy."

Lance nuzzled her cheek with the soft hair of his beard. "Mm-hmm. Spreadsheets. Alphabetized file folders."

Her laughter rang through the foyer. "Irresistible, dear."

Lance kissed her softly. "Go. I'll hold down the fort. You'll be glad you took a nap when Andi and Hawthorne want to stay up late playing board games."

Daisy nodded. He was right. She might be exhausted, but she wanted to soak in every minute of Andi being here while it lasted. She'd been hurt when her twin told her of the plans to move back to Virginia and start a security firm with Agent McClain, but the way Ross brought out the laughter in Andi's eyes was hard to argue with.

She was glad her twin had found someone to share her life with. Daisy glanced back at her husband, who was now happily sorting stacks of Post-It notes and credit card slips. If it was anything like her life with Lance, Andi was at the beginning of quite the adventure.

Poppy pulled on the oversized waffle-knit sweater. It wasn't the fanciest look, but this was her family, and she was determined to enjoy every bit of casual she could before she was officially the Second Lady.

And Harrison became Vice President of the United States.

"Maggie is looking for her brown boot. Do you know where it is?"

The question made her smile. "I think Henry might have stashed it in the oven of his kitchen."

Harrison chuckled. "Okay then." He took one step and then turned back. "You look lovely, by the way." He left without waiting for a response.

She flushed with pleasure. Poppy knew that Harrison liked her just as well in ball gowns or sweatpants.

A moment later, she raised her eyebrow as Harrison reappeared. "That wasn't the right boot. She wants the one with the pink laces."

Magnolia was nothing if not opinionated. She was like her parents in that way.

"Did you check the van? If it's not there, tell her she has to find another pair."

Harrison disappeared again and Poppy laughed. Such an important task for the future VP.

Now that the threats from the ALA were taken care of and the election was over, Poppy was face to face with the reality that this was really happening.

When he came back, Harrison slipped his hands

around her waist. "Success. Both kids are dressed, brushed, and ready to go."

"Very impressive." Their reflection in the mirror showed a picture she'd seen a thousand times. But sometimes, she still felt like they should be the awkward teenagers smiling for a graduation photo.

"Did I mention you look beautiful?"

"You did, but feel free to do it again," she teased.

"Well, it's true." He kissed her temple. "Are you ready for our next adventure?"

Poppy turned to face him, still trapped in his embrace. "You know I am."

"Do you think I'm ready?" The vulnerability of his question was one of the reasons Poppy loved this man so deeply. Harrison was strong and confident and incredibly gifted. He was genuine with everyone, but there was a side of him that only Poppy knew.

"Yes, you are. But even if you aren't—God's calling you to do it anyway. And He'll equip you."

They'd had this conversation before, but Poppy didn't mind being the one to reassure her husband.

He nodded and kissed her. "I love you."

"I love you too."

"I don't know where I'd be without you."

Poppy kissed him again before stepping back. "Guess we'll never know."

She checked her watch. "We'd better go. If we're late, Hawthorne will blame us for holding up dinner."

LAVENDER FINISHED ADJUSTING the lighting on the photo she'd taken in her Grateful for Jesus shirt and uploaded them to her social media profiles.

"You ready?" Emmett poked his head in, holding Caleb. The fourteen-month old was reaching for her as soon as he saw her.

"Yep. Just finished." She pulled Caleb into her arms and kissed his forehead. "Hey, sweet boy. You ready for some turkey?"

"Mama!"

"I'm ready for some pie," Emmett replied.

She grinned. "You might have to wrestle Josh for it. Remember last year?"

Her husband nodded. "Oh, I remember. I've been practicing my paper football skills."

She narrowed her eyes. "Is that what you do when you're supposed to be writing?"

"Thinking *is* writing, dear."

"Mmm-hmm. If you say so." They were both authors, but the depths of Emmett's creativity continued to astound her. Her books were straightforward—nonfiction and devotional books for women and teenagers. But his? The worlds he dreamed up were incredible. "And how is your book coming? Your deadline is... next month?"

Emmett shrugged. "It's wandering a bit. I think I like where it is going, but it's not there yet."

Lavender leaned forward and kissed him. "Not all who wander are lost."

He perked up at the invitation to their ongoing game. "Too easy, love. That's Tolkein."

She shrugged. "Fair enough. You're up."

"I've got one to stump you, but it'll have to wait. There's a pie with my name on it."

Caleb clapped. "Paaa!"

She gasped.

Emmett grinned at their little boy. "Yeah, buddy! You want some pie?"

Lavender bounced Caleb, and they started down the steps. After they'd tried so hard to have children, she would never fail to marvel at the gift she'd been given in her little family. Caleb, so bright and cheerful was the perfect addition.

She buckled him into the car seat and walked

around the rear of the small SUV. Emmett tugged her hand and pulled her into his arms. "Hey, beautiful."

"I love you," she said in response, tipping her head up for a kiss.

LILY MOVED through the living room, quickly picking up toys and the dirty outfit Maia had left lying around as she got ready for Thanksgiving dinner.

Josh walked in, toothbrush in hand. He glanced around the room before looking back at her with a sneaky grin. "What do you think about a four-wheeler for Maia for Christmas?"

Lily felt her jaw drop. "You can't be serious, Josh!"

"Come on. She's five, almost six! They've got little ones. It could even be pink."

He looked so excited by the prospect, and his earnest look had Lily shaking her head. "I'm not prepared to have this conversation right now."

He stuck his toothbrush in his mouth and spoke around it. "We'll talk later. I'm telling you, this is a great idea."

Lily laughed. "Yeah, well—that's debatable." Lily knew her first instinct would always be the straight-laced, safe option. But she also knew that she and Josh found the perfect balance. She still wasn't sure if he'd talk her into the four-wheeler this year, but she'd go into the discussion with an open mind. Mostly.

Maia, her beautiful adopted daughter, came into the living room with a stack of books. "Can I bring these in the car?"

Lily chuckled. "Sure. But we're just going to Grandma and Grandpa's house. It's a two-minute drive."

"I might get bored," Maia replied matter-of-factly. The quiet, timid girl she'd been when she was first adopted 18 months ago had transformed into a quietly confident kindergartener this fall. Lily couldn't imagine life without her.

Or Josh.

She'd fought against his pursuit for so long, but now she savored the way he loved her without reservation.

"Are you ready, munchkin?" Josh grabbed Maia under the arms and flipped her up over his shoulder, tickling her ribs for good measure. Her laughter rang through the living room and Lily smiled as she tucked toys into bins. "You didn't pay the bridge troll!"

"Maia, when the troll lets you down, go get in the car and get buckled."

Josh set her down and stepped toward Lily with a mischievous grin.

Lily put on her best disapproving look, but she couldn't fight the grin that spread across her face. Josh's hands found their mark under her arms and she squealed.

"Joshua Elliot, stop that!"

He laughed and paused his assault, wrapping her in a hug instead. She looked up at him and he pressed a kiss to her lips that made her stomach flip. It still amazed her that this man loved her so deeply.

"We're going to be late," she said chidingly. "Mom's going to give me that look."

"I'll take the blame. Your mom loves me." He kissed her again, deeper this time. "But... Maia is waiting for us too. I love you."

"And I love you," she said.

He held out his hand in front of them. "After you." She started to walk and his eyes fell to her hands with a spark of laughter. "You can probably leave the laundry here though."

She threw their daughter's dirty clothes at him

with a grin and scurried toward the garage as he chased after her.

ROSE HUNG up the phone as Tate stepped into her old bedroom, still damp from the shower he'd just taken.

"That was Kenny, checking in." Their foreman was holding down the fort at Rose Ridge Ranch while they made the visit back to Indiana.

"Everything okay?"

She nodded. "Yep. I guess the western well pump went out, but he said Grainger is coming out to take a look at it tomorrow. I hope he knows where to find the spare tank." Rose frowned at her phone. She hated being away from her animals. But she loved being home. Two full years she'd been in Montana, and it hadn't gotten any easier.

Tate wrapped his arms around her from behind and she leaned back into him. "Don't worry. Kenny's got things covered."

She sighed. "I know."

He chuckled. "Do you want to call him back?"

Rose rolled her shoulders back. "No. No, he's

fine. He knows his stuff. And we're here. And I'm going to just enjoy being here."

"I think that's good," Tate replied.

When he didn't say anything else, Rose glanced back at her phone. "I'm just going to text him."

She sent Kenny a reminder about the tank he could haul water with. When she was done, Tate held out his hand, palm up.

She pulled her mouth to one side in a pout, then set her phone in his hand. He slipped it into his pocket. "I promise I'll give this to you if he needs something."

She stepped back into Tate's arms. "Thanks, Cowboy."

"Anytime."

"Is it strange for you to be back here?" Tate had lived at Bloom's Farm for five years before leaving to take over his family ranch in Montana.

He shook his head. "No. Not strange. I guess I still sort of feel like I should be sleeping in a trailer parked in the pasture. But other than that, it's just nice to be back." His hands rubbed her back in a gentle massage. "Besides, I learned long ago that wherever I'm with you feels like home. So I'm good."

Rose smiled and tipped her head up to look at him. "I feel the same way."

He dropped a kiss on her lips, exploring leisurely until they both stepped back at the sound of new voices upstairs.

"I guess we should head up," Tate suggested.

"Probably. I love you, Cowboy."

"Love you more."

ANDI BUSIED herself setting the table as Ross charmed her mother and father. He'd been at the house since ten this morning. He and Tate had already bonded over the pros and cons of Angus steers.

She watched with pride as Ross carried on an effortless conversation with her dad. Something about Civil War politics. The accomplished Secret Service agent somehow fit right in here at their Thanksgiving dinner.

If she had known their less-than-ideal meeting at the dojo would end like this, perhaps she would have handled it differently. Of course, if she had acted differently, perhaps it would never have ended like this.

It didn't really matter though. Andi was finally beginning to accept that she could claw and fight for control. Or she could trust that God had it taken care of. She'd spent the last year trying to determine her own next steps, when what she really needed was to let God guide her path. What was that saying she'd heard? To ask God for just enough light for the step she was on.

It certainly seemed like that was the prayer she needed as she and Ross started a security firm. If Black Tower Security was going to be what they'd envisioned, she couldn't micromanage it and keep it in a neat little box. She needed just enough guidance to know the next step.

Ross stood up. "Need any help?"

"Sure. We still need silverware in the second dining room, and you can put napkins on the kids' table."

"Sir, yes, sir," he said with a wink.

She smiled.

There was no one she would rather take it one step at a time with than the man next to her. She knew an engagement was coming soon, though she was desperately trying not to control what was supposed to be a sweet surprise. It would come when it was time and not before.

"I love you, Ross."

A crooked grin crossed his face. "I love you too."

LAURA BLOOM SQUEEZED her husband's hand. Dinner had been cleaned up, and pie had been served. She'd ordered them from the bakery in Minden this year instead of making her own. It was simply that each year the crowd had grown, and her stamina had waned.

But she knew it wasn't the food that mattered.

What mattered was the way Lance laid a protective hand on Daisy's arm as she leaned to pick up a napkin. And the way Hawthorne had blessed the meal and talked to God like he was talking to a friend. What mattered was her family—blessed and thankful and following God. It was everything she'd ever prayed for each of them.

Next week, Rose and Tate would return to Montana. And Andi and Ross would go back to Virginia. Poppy and Harrison would officially transition to Washington DC.

Once again, her family would be scattered across the country, separated by thousands of miles. But for right now, in this moment, they were all together.

"I'd like to say something," she said.

She might not command a room like the next vice president or a sergeant major, but if she'd taught her children anything, it was to listen when mom was talking.

Quickly, silence fell around the room as her children shushed one another and her grandchildren.

"I'd like a moment. I'm not much for talking to a crowd, but well—sometimes God puts something on your heart you can't help but share."

She stood in the doorway between the two dining rooms, her gaze sliding from person to person as she spoke.

"In 1982, your father and I bought this property with a dream. A small family farm where we could live on our own terms. Where we could raise our children to love the Lord and love the land. There were four of us at the time. Lily," she turned to her oldest daughter, "when we showed you your new home, you cried for a week. Hawthorne—I think you slept outside under the stars for nearly a month."

Chuckles broke out around the room.

"Then Daisy and Dandelion came along and we knew we'd made the right decision. Poppy, Lavender, Rose... Each of you brought something new and special to this family and this farm. And watching each of you grow up has been the greatest joy of our lives."

She felt the sting of tears in her eyes. "And now, instead of seven children, I have fourteen!"

"I don't see a ring yet," Hawthorne yelled.

Laura laughed. "Yes, well—let's just say I'm not afraid to count my chickens in this case." Ross had asked them for permission this morning while Andi was in the shower. "What I'm trying to say—before I was interrupted—" she gave a lighthearted look of ire at Hawthorne, "is that I'm so very proud of each and every one of you. I thank God every day that he chose me to be your mother."

Tears were rolling down her face now, and she wiped them with a napkin before sitting back down. "That's all."

"For crying out loud, Mom. Did you have to go and make us all cry?" Lavender dabbed at her eyes with a napkin.

Daisy chimed in next. "Pregnant woman here! I was already crying because my pie was gone, and then you had to go get all sentimental."

Laura laughed through the tears. Before she knew it, she was surrounded by the arms of her children.

"We love you, Mom."

Agreement echoed through the room. "We're the lucky ones, Mom."

"Love you, Grandma."

Her heart lifted a prayer of thanksgiving to the Lord for entrusting her with these children for all these years. And she asked for many, many additional years to enjoy them all the more.

THE END

Note to Readers

NOTE TO READERS

Thank you for picking up (or downloading!) this book. If you enjoyed it, please consider taking a minute to leave a review or rating.

I waited a long time to tell Dandelion's story. Along the way, I got to understand her deeper than I imagined. She's tough, with a deep desire to prove herself. She feels deeply, but doesn't express those emotions readily. But I loved seeing how Ross softened her rough edges. And I especially loved watching them both give up their desire for control to allow God to shape their future.

Speaking of God's provision...I had huge dreams for this series, and God has surpassed every single one. My original plans for this series were for all seven books to be released in one year – 2020, hah!

God had other plans, and even before COVID changed the world, he called me to bring my kids home full-time. The Bloom Sisters then became a two-year endeavor, but I wouldn't change a thing.

I hope you have loved this family as much as I have. Laura is the mother I hope to be someday — patient and kind and, most of all, prayerful. She has a quiet strength that allows her to hold this family together. And each sibling carries a little piece of my heart. Hawthorne with his tentative steps of courage, Daisy with her creative spirit, Poppy with her idealistic convictions, Lavender with her insecurities, Lily with her wounded heart, Rose with her ambitious goals, and Dandelion with her hidden depths.

Perhaps you have a specific family member who you connected with! I would love to know. I pray my books encourage you in your faith and through your struggles, whatever they may be. I love hearing the amazing ways God has used my words in the lives of my readers. It is incredibly humbling and encouraging! You can email me anytime at taragraceericson@gmail.com.

In case you are wondering — we will see more of Andi and Ross in my upcoming romantic suspense series. And, if you are eager to see more of Minden (including some time at Bloom's Farm!), I'll have more news about the upcoming Second Chance Fire Station Series soon!

You can learn more about my upcoming projects at my website: www.taragraceericson.com or by signing up for my newsletter. Just for signing up, you'll get two free stories, including Clean Slate, the introduction to the Black Tower Security Series. It's the story of what happened with Ross's friend Jessica while he was busy in Indiana! Sign up to start reading it today.

If you've never read my other books, I'd love for you to read the Main Street Minden Series and dive into the world of Minden, Indiana.

Thank you again for all your support and encouragement.

-Tara

ACKNOWLEDGMENTS

The sheer number of people to thank for their support of this book and this series is overwhelming.

Above all – Thank you, God. Without Your blessings and direction, these books would never exist. You are so incredibly faithful. I offer all these words and those to come to You for Your purposes.

A super special thank you goes to Britney Dahlkoetter, for graciously allowing me to pick your brain about Andi's Army experience, and draw from your own career! In some cases, I took creative license to make the story work, but any errors are entirely my own, and I am so grateful for your help– and your service!

To my editor, Jessica from BH Writing Services.

This series has been a journey for both of us. Through hard times, lonely times, and fun times – I am glad we got to do it together.

To Hannah Jo Abbott and Mandi Blake, for being the best accountability, prayer, and venting partners a girl could ask for.

And to the rest of our Author Circle -- Jess Mastorakos, Elizabeth Maddrey and K Leah. Iron sharpens iron... and entertains one another on long days with strings of messages thousands of lines long.

To Gabbi. Because best friends are sisters from God.

To my parents, for being a wonderful example of love, faith, and hard work. Especially to my mother, for being my extra set of eyes (and ears) for every story!

Thank you to all my readers, without whose support and encouragement, I would have given up a long time ago.

An extra special thank you to the members of my launch team. Your reviews, photos, feedback, encouragement, and enthusiasm make release day and beyond so much more fun. None of you had any real idea what you were getting into when you signed up for this team, but I'm thrilled you've stuck with me through all seven books! And I'm overjoyed to now count you among my friends. I value each of your opinions and so appreciate your candid feedback.

Abbi from @adventuresofaliterarynature
Ashley from @bringingupbooks
Kim from @inspirationalfictionreader
Kristin from @books_faith_love
Kristina from @blessednbookish
Mimi from @books.n.blossoms
Nicole from @nicole.and.the.unending.tbr
Rebecca from @adventure_through_the_pages
Rose from @adventurousbookworm
Sheila from @reading_with_belle

And to all the other bloggers, bookstagrammers, and reviewers who read my books and share your thoughts. Thank you from the bottom of my heart.

And finally, to my husband. You'll probably never read these words, since you don't read my books. But you do dishes and laundry and make me laugh more than any other human. So I'll take it. I'd choose you again a million times.

Mr. B – Your sweet little heart melts mine.

Little C – My heart can talk to yours with no words at all. But watching you find your words is a beautiful thing.

And Baby L – Whenever you're ready to sleep through the night... I'm here for it. Love you, sweet boy.

Clean Slate

Curious about Ross's friend who was in trouble during the book?

Read Clean Slate for free today by signing up for Tara's newsletter and get a taste of the full-length romantic suspense series. Download it today!

She's running for her life. He can't lose her again.

Personal trainer Jessica Street has stumbled into a money laundering scheme at her gym, and the people responsible aren't too happy about the extra liability. To make matters worse, the only person who

can help her is the one man she never wants to see again.

Flint Raven regrets breaking Jessica's heart ten years ago when he chose his career over her. But the former security tech mogul isn't the man he used to be. When bullets start flying, he knows he'll do anything to protect her and prove he's worthy of a second chance.

Jessica has no choice to accept his help. But she's determined to protect her heart while Flint is protecting her life.

Potential Threat

Black Tower Security Book 1 - Potential Threat.

Can this bad-boy bodyguard protect America's sweetheart without losing *his* heart?

Fiona Raven is famous for her homestyle cooking with a hint of Italian flair. Everyone knows her face and has her pre-packaged food in their freezer. So why is she receiving threatening notes? Fiona's brother insists on sending a bodyguard, news that only gets worse when she realizes it is his friend Ryder - the one man she could never let herself love.

Ryder McClain has played the villain enough times to appreciate being the hero working for Black Tower Security. Along with his new client comes a stern warning from her brother - his boss and best friend - to keep his hands off. It doesn't matter anyway, Fiona is the perfect woman, and exactly the kind he doesn't deserve.

Ryder will do whatever it takes to protect Fiona. Threatening notes turn into suspicious break-ins and destructive corporate espionage, and this bodyguard assignment gets even more serious. Can Ryder get to the bottom of the threat before his heart gets too involved?

Order Potential Threat today!

ABOUT THE AUTHOR

Tara Grace Ericson lives in Missouri with her husband and three sons. She studied engineering and worked as an engineer for many years before embracing her creative side to become a full-time author. Now, she spends her days chasing her boys and writing books when she can.

She loves cooking, crocheting, and reading books by the dozen. She loves a good "happily ever after" with an engaging love story. That's why Tara focuses on writing clean contemporary romance, with an emphasis on Christian faith and living. She wants to encourage her readers with stories of men and women who live out their faith in tough situations.

BOOKS BY TARA GRACE ERICSON

Free Stories

Love and Chocolate

Clean Slate (Romantic Suspense)

The Main Street Minden Series

Falling on Main Street

Winter Wishes

Spring Fever

Summer to Remember

Kissing in the Kitchen: A Main Street Minden Novella

The Bloom Sisters Series

Hoping for Hawthorne - A Bloom Family Novella

A Date for Daisy

Poppy's Proposal

Lavender and Lace

Longing for Lily

Resisting Rose

Black Tower Security

Potential Threat

Made in the USA
Middletown, DE
15 January 2022